Bye Baby
Louise Collins
Copyright © 2021
Cover by Books and moods
Edited by Sandra at http://oneloveediting.com/

FLOWERSHOP ASSASSINS

Dedication

This is for anyone who needs cheering up.
I hope Bye Baby makes you smile, and you can escape real life reading about Donnie and Elliot's ridiculous antics.
It's fun, fast and not to be taken too seriously.
I really enjoyed writing this one and love my flower shop assassins.
I'll be celebrating release day/commiserating turning 30 with a glass of bubbles, and a tub or two of ice cream.
I won't be standing on the scales for at least a month, if ever again…

Happy Reading!

Louise <3

CHAPTER ONE

Donnie limped along the pavement, one of his heels pinched with a blister. He didn't care enough to look why it hurt; he had tunnel vision, eyes on the flower shop at the end of the street. The bright flowers in the window and the sun's glare were too much for his stinging eyes, but he kept on going, blinking back the dryness.

Donnie could vaguely hear children playing in the nearby park. Something sharp twisted in his stomach. He blocked the sound out and kept on trudging along the path.

He pushed open the door, and the bell rang, drawing attention to him. Yates, behind the counter, glared. A shadow of something passed in his eyes, but he went back to serving an old lady.

Her long trench coat hung down to the floor, and she wore a woven hat. She smelled so strongly of nauseating lavender, Donnie shoved his face into a bucket of roses.

Yates was serving her, smiling away his dark demeanor. He even wore a floral shirt to go with the whole flower shop façade, but Donnie knew what lay under that shirt—a six-pack the old lady would've fainted over, scars that each had a story, and a patchwork of tattoos, none of which were flowers.

Yates spoke in low tones, a soft rumble to the woman who was taking far too long to buy a lily and asking far too many questions about how to keep it alive.

Fuck the lily—with how old she looked, she should've been thinking about herself.

Donnie knew he wasn't going to get the same voice from Yates. The rumble would be threatening like approaching thunder.

The woman took her lily off the counter and thanked Yates, who smiled and waved. A complete lie—he was a mean bastard really, an asshole with a sadistic kink. If the old lady knew his bedside manner, she would've had a heart attack right there and then.

The old lady turned to leave and froze when she saw Donnie by the door. She hugged her lily close to her side, giving him a distasteful look up and down.

"Problem?"

Her wrinkled mouth stammered open. "N—No, it's just…"

She held the lily with one hand and reached into her pocket with her other. Donnie raised his eyebrows at the jangle of change when she presented him with a few coins.

"Get yourself a coffee."

Yates folded his arms, shaking his head and flaring his nostrils, all obvious signals he did not want Donnie to take the old woman's money.

Donnie held his hand out, smiling. "Thank you."

She grinned back, then passed through the door. He waited until he could no longer see her, then turned the sign on the front door to Closed. He looked at the coins in his palm.

"There's enough for two. You want one?"

"Get the fuck out," Yates growled.

Donnie shook his head. "I want a job."

"You're in no fit state for a job."

"I'm fine."

"You said you were fine last time."

"Last time I was lying."

Yates's hand came crashing down on the counter. "You're not fine. You're a wreck, Donnie, and I'm so close to killing you right now."

He shook his head. "I need a job—"

"Yes, a normal job. You're washed up. Go to the job center; they'll sort you something out, get you on a program too."

"I don't need to go on a program."

"How much have you had to drink this morning?"

Donnie looked up at the ceiling, pondering. "When does last night become this morning? Is midnight last thing at night, or first thing in the morning. What would you say?"

He looked at Yates for an answer, but he gave him a cold stare instead.

"It was just a thought."

Yates huffed, wiping his hand down his face. "Jesus. The only reason I haven't gone over there and punched your teeth in is because people can see inside the shop."

"I could lower the blinds."

"Don't tempt me."

"I need this."

Yates shook his head.

Donnie pressed his hands together. "You want me to beg, I'll beg."

"Are you serious right now?"

"Yes."

Yates widened his eyes. "Where's the ruthless, stylish man I remember? Where's the aggression and flair."

"He's gone."

"Where's your dignity?"

Donnie lowered his hands. "I don't have any anymore, okay. I need—"

"You're not fit for a job. Look at you!"

Donnie couldn't even remember what he'd put on that morning, and he didn't take a second to look. Instead he stared at Yates, growing more annoyed at the bright flowers hurting his eyes. "Fashion advice from a guy in a floral shirt."

"I can smell you from here."

"And I smell fucking amazing."

"No you don't. You put your head in that," Yates said, pointing.

Donnie held up his hands. "She smelled like lavender, strong lavender—it makes me nauseous. I couldn't handle it, but I can handle the smell of roses."

"Roses? You shoved your face in a trash can."

Donnie looked at it. The flowers seemed blurry, unfocused, but he'd been certain. "Roses?"

"They're printed on the outside of the can. It's full of stem clippings and my leftover breakfast."

"It still smells better than lavender."

Yates slammed his fist down again, knocking a pair of scissors to the floor. "Have you even looked at your feet?"

Donnie sighed, tilted his head forward, then looked at them. "Ha, look at that. I've still got two."

"Your shoes don't match."

"Who are you, the shoe police?"

"You've lost it."

"You still give Ranger jobs."

"Ranger completes them!"

"I fucked up. That's why I'm like…" Donnie frowned. "What I'm like," he finished, gesturing to himself.

"We're done here."

Yates folded his arms and gave Donnie the deadly, silent-fury look that built in the atmosphere and stole all the air.

A month ago Donnie would've backed away, but despite him making light of it, he knew he'd hit rock bottom and needed Yates's help.

"Please."

Yates stopped glaring and relaxed his deadly stance.

Donnie used to have the same glare, that same deadly stance. He was a shadow of his former self and hated it.

"One job to prove I'm not washed up. One job to prove myself again. I know I've messed up; I've let myself slip, but I really need this. This is all I've ever been good at."

"That's the problem. You were good—you were the best in the business, but you're not anymore."

"I know," Donnie said. "Just one, please."

Yates closed his eyes and cursed under his breath.

"You think I'm happy about being this?" Donnie said, tugging the hem of his jacket. He didn't even remember putting one on that morning, but apparently, he had. "You think I don't know what—who—I was, and what I am now? That's why I'm asking for your help."

Yates slowly opened his eyes, and his lips twisted into a frightening grin. Donnie had no idea what it meant, but he knew it wasn't good. He came out from behind the counter and stood in front of it.

"Prove how far you've fallen, how you've got no dignity. Crawl across the floor and kiss my feet."

"Have you lost your mind!"

"Apparently you have, so prove it. I want Donnie King to crawl across the floor and kiss my feet."

"This some kind of sick fantasy of yours?"

"Not really, but I probably will jerk off to it later."

"There's no way—"

"Then there's no job for you."

Donnie clutched his hair and released a snarl. "I'll kill you one day for this."

"Less threats, more feet action."

"Fuck you," Donnie said, dropping to his knees. His face flamed, but he shuffled one knee in front of the other and made his way across the floor to Yates. Yates smiled down at him, chest puffed out, clearly getting some kind of sexual kick out of Donnie on his knees.

Donnie stared at his reflected face in Yates's shoes, then leaned down, pressing a kiss to the leather.

Yates kicked him away. "No more. My shoes are clean…you're not."

"I did what you asked."

Yates pointed to the door. "Lock it and come into the back."

Donnie got to his feet, locked the door, then rushed after Yates into the office. He stood one side of the desk, while Yates sat the other. He'd actually missed being in there, missed these moments when he heard a name.

"I better not end up regretting this."

"You won't, I swear."

"But you must be desperate if you'd kiss my fucking shoes, so here's me, giving my one shit about you."

Donnie watched as Yates unlocked the desk drawer, then pulled out a fat folder with the name Elliot Austin printed on the front.

"This was one of mine," Yates said. "I was planning on doing it tonight. I've got his address. I know when he'll be in. I know where the cameras are around the perimeter and a safe place to park the car."

Donnie nodded along. "Okay."

"It's an easy kill. That old woman hobbling down the road could do it, understand?"

"I understand. How much?"

"It's a 50K hit."

Donnie chuckled, imagining all he could buy with 50K.

"I'm taking fifty percent," Yates muttered.

"What? Why?"

He jabbed his finger down on the folder. "Because I've done all the legwork. I'm giving him to you as a favor on the agreement that with your share you get yourself sorted out."

"I'm sure I'll get sorted out."

Yates flared his nostrils. "I don't mean drugs, I don't mean drink, and I don't mean dick. I want you to use the money to get your goddamn head together. You crawled across the floor and kissed my goddamn shoes."

"Let's never mention that again," Donnie said, raising his hands. "Do you have a photograph?"

Yates rolled his eyes. "Of course I have a photograph."

He flipped open the folder, then handed one to Donnie.

"Elliot Austin. Twenty-three."

Sandy-blond hair, baby blue eyes that burned the camera, and a confident smile on his lips. He stood on a sidewalk wearing denim shorts and an open turquoise shirt, flashing his firm stomach.

Donnie swallowed hard.

"You listening!"

"Sorry, what?"

Yates held out a piece of paper to him. "Here's his address. He's been living there a month. This is his schedule. He goes to the gym Tuesdays, will be back at his apartment at 20:30."

"Got it," Donnie said.

Yates handed him another piece of paper. A bird's-eye view of the apartment block and the surrounding areas. "I've marked up where the cameras are, and a good place to leave the car. I've even highlighted the route I was going to use to get from the car to the address. Quiet alleys. The code to the building is 4567, and there's a camera pointed at the door, but I'm sure you can handle it since I've done every goddamn thing else."

Yates stopped to breathe. "Got all that?"

"Yeah, I've got it. Any specific method?"

"No. The client didn't have any specific requirements for the kill, but I will say the apartments are low-budget, thin walls. I'd advise quieter methods. Smothering, strangulation, stabbing. You don't look like you could get away if the police came after you."

"That's a bit harsh."

"Don't get drunk."

Donnie scoffed. "What do you take me for?"

"A drunk. Would've thought that was fairly obvious."

"I won't let you down."

"Let me down, I put you down."

"What?"

"I mean it. You're a liability to me and this business. You mess this up and I will kill you."

Donnie looked down at his feet. "I mess this up and I deserve to die."

"No one else would've given you their easy hit. I don't want to kill you. I actually quite like you."

"You and Ranger are my closest friends."

"And that's disturbing considering I just made you kiss my shoes, then threatened to kill you."

"Don't pretend you're not into that."

Yates laughed. The hair at the back of Donnie's neck stood up.

"Oh, and if Ranger asks, you did all the legwork. Can't have him screaming favoritism."

"My lips are sealed."

Yates waved him away. "Now go sober up, get ready, and kill this man."

****

Donnie thought he'd hit rock bottom, but apparently it was only a trapdoor to worse horrors.

He'd crawled across the floor of the flower shop to kiss Yates's shoes.

Him, Donnie King, assassin extraordinaire, hot, sexy, ruthless, efficient, or at least he used to be. Now he shoved his head in trash cans, begged like a dog, and kissed shoes.

Not for much longer.

Elliot Austin was going to pull him from his rut.

His photo, his details, and the map were laid out on his coffee table, and Donnie had gone over them again and again.

He'd packed knives, duct tape, a spray can, and a lock pick in a backpack, his killing kit.

It all looked easy. There was no specific method chosen, and Donnie was going to see where the mood took him, what was available at the time, and what state he found Elliot in.

The last two hits had been utter disasters. He prayed for a third time lucky.

He got up, went into the bathroom, and forced himself to look into the mirror. His tangled hair dropped down to his shoulders, and he couldn't remember the last time he'd washed it. His beard was all uneven and wild, and he didn't blame the old lady for thinking he was a homeless man.

Donnie didn't like the whiskey-stained T-shirt he was wearing, or the worn leather jacket, but his old clothes didn't fit anymore. He'd let himself go, let his physique slip, and although he didn't like what stared back at him in the mirror, he had zero motivation to change it.

He looked like he hadn't slept in days, which he found odd—all he did was sleep and drink. He swore his eyes had changed color from deep brown to the amber of whiskey.

"Time to go," he said to himself, backing away from the sink.

He left the bathroom, shoved Elliot's info into his backpack, then went to leave. He paused in front of the door, arm outstretched, ready to go. His hands had a permanent tremble, and the shakes only got worse when he watched.

He needed to get there early, make sure Elliot went inside the apartment before killing him when it was quiet, which meant a lot of time waiting around doing nothing.

He once enjoyed the waiting, the anticipation, that little hit of nervousness mixed with the desire to fulfill his duty, but he didn't like the waiting anymore.

The waiting led to second-guessing, fears of failure, fears of fucking up, and god forbid, his messed-up memories. Donnie couldn't stand waiting.

Donnie turned his head, and his gaze found the whiskey bottle on the side. Yates would kill him if he found out, but if it all went well, there'd be no way he'd know.

It would be a secret between him and the bottle.

Donnie grabbed it and left.

CHAPTER TWO

Yates knew his stuff.

Elliot Austin arrived at his apartment block at 20:30. He was wearing sweatpants and a matching zip-up top. He had a backpack on his back and stared down at his phone as he walked along.

Donnie licked his lips, then gave in to temptation, swigging another mouthful of whiskey from the bottle. He'd drank so much the burn no longer registered, and his taste buds were well and truly fucked.

He stood on the other side of the road, hiding in the shadows. Elliot hadn't noticed death lurking nearby. He'd walked up to the keypad and prodded in the code.

To be an effective assassin, you had to be invisible, had to make sure the mark was completely unaware. Donnie had always been good at blending in.

He went to shove the bottle back into his backpack, but where the shadows aided him to stay hidden, they didn't help with him trying to get a wide bottle through a small drawstring hole.

"Shit," he hissed.

The bottle slipped, and he didn't have the reflexes to catch it. He watched it fall to the pavement in slow motion. Before it hit the ground, he ducked, crouching down to hide behind the car parked on the road in front of him. He may not have had the reflexes to catch the bottle, but he could drop to the ground like a ninja when needed.

The bottle smashed, spraying him with whiskey droplets and glass.

Donnie gritted his teeth, waiting for Elliot to investigate. He tugged the traitorous hole of the bag wider, then reached for one of his switchblades.

It wasn't going to be the clean kill Yates had prepared for, but Donnie was still going to take Elliot out. There were a few people dotted about, but it was dark and cold which acted as another deterrent. As soon as Elliot poked his head around the car to see where the sound had come from, Donnie was going to stick him with the knife.

Once, twice—no, three times to be certain.

He'd drag him down the alley he'd come from, then leave him there to bleed out. Not clean, not stylish, not one to be proud of, but at least it would be done.

Donnie got ready to strike like a viper, like a scorpion with its stinger ready for action, except no one came peeking over the car.

He didn't hear any footsteps coming closer either.

Donnie stood slowly from his crouch. Elliot wasn't standing in front of the apartment block anymore, but the door was slowly closing, as if someone had passed through.

"Thank you, god," he muttered.

He hadn't blown it, but next came the waiting. He hated waiting, and even though the whiskey had almost messed it up for him, he couldn't resist another mouthful…or two.

****

It was time.

Donnie grabbed the spray can from his backpack, made sure there were no cars or people in the vicinity, then rushed across the road. He thought about smashing the camera, but it was low enough for the spray can to effectively take it out.

After he'd taken care of the camera, he typed in the keypad code.

Elliot lived on the ground floor, which was a massive blessing, Donnie couldn't handle flights of stairs in his state. Even walking down the corridor was a struggle, but he found the right door and dropped with a thud to his knees.

He'd been lock picking since he was a kid, had a knack for it, but that had been before he'd messed up, before he'd started drinking heavily, before he'd got the tremor in his hands.

Donnie could barely see the keyhole he was trying to get the pick into. The metal caught, making a pinging sound, and scraped, making him wince. He cursed under his breath, trying and trying, and eventually the lock clunked.

Donnie pocketed the lock pick, swung his backpack onto his shoulder, and opened the door.

He didn't have time to blink or duck or even prepare for what came at his face.

It hit him hard, and all went dark.

****

Donnie tasted blood first. The metallic twang on his palate. He'd thought the whiskey had destroyed all his taste buds, but he'd been wrong.

He groaned as he opened his eyes, taking a few vital seconds to adjust to the room. He scrunched up his nose, noting the tightness and the trickle of blood his movement released. He was in a living room, could see a sofa, a TV, a table, a kitchen. Nothing personal on the walls, no ornaments, just a bland apartment space.

Donnie tried to move, but he'd been bound. Ropes secured his ankles and thighs to the legs of it, and his wrists and elbows were tied behind him. One more rope secured his chest to the chair. All in all, Donnie couldn't do anything but wriggle and grunt. His muscles were all cramping, and his shoulders burned in their bent-back position.

"You're awake, then?"

Elliot Austin. Blond hair, blue eyes, and an amused smile. He came into the room holding two backpacks and set them down on the floor.

"I'm awake."

Elliot moved to the sofa and picked up a frying pan of all things. He showed the bottom of the pan to Donnie, all covered in blood.

"That's what you hit me with…"

Elliot nodded, then held the frying pan like a baseball bat. He swung it, then lifted it in the air like he was celebrating a home run.

"You went down like a sack of shit."

"Isn't the term, 'like a sack of potatoes'?"

"For most people, yeah." Elliot dropped the pan on the sofa. "Had to drag you in here, get you on that chair—no easy feat. Did my back in."

"I'm sorry I was so difficult."

"You were hired to kill me?"

Donnie clacked his tongue to the roof of his mouth. "Yeah."

"I gotta say, I was hoping for more. No offense."

"I am slightly offended."

Elliot snorted. "So I'm guessing you know my name?"

"Yeah."

"Can I know yours?"

"Donnie," he sighed.

"Wait," Elliot said, wagging a finger. "Are you Donnie King?"

"The one and—"

"No, you can't be."

"Why not?"

"I heard Donnie King was the best, no man he can't kill. And he's supposed to be seriously hot—like get an inappropriate hard-on before he kills you kinda hot."

Donnie looked away. "Now you're just being mean."

"What was the plan exactly?"

"I hadn't really thought about it."

Elliot narrowed his eyes. "Aren't you supposed to plan your hits?"

"I'm an expert. I don't need to."

"There's a certain kitchen utensil that says otherwise."

"How did you know I was coming?"

Elliot hummed. "Well, let's see. First, I heard something smash outside, and looked over to see a strange man lowering himself to the ground."

"I dropped down so fast, nothing but a blur—"

"No you didn't."

"Fuck."

"I thought that was a bit odd but carried on inside the building. Then at midnight I was woken by the sound of a cat trying to get into the apartment, which was even odder because I don't have a cat. I stood waiting with the frying pan, but you were taking so long, I took pity on you and opened the door."

"I picked the lock."

"Sorry, but you didn't."

"Shit," Donnie said, shuffling in his chair. He shouldn't have brought the bottle along; he should've kept a clear head.

"Shit indeed. What was it that smashed outside?"

"Whiskey."

"There's definitely a whiskey smell about you."

"Now what?"

"Well, let's see what we got," Elliot said, opening one of the backpacks. Donnie realized it was his.

"Spray can, knives, duct tape, cable ties. How old-school."

He picked up one of the flick knives and opened it. The small clicking sound punctured the air, and Donnie knew he'd had it. He'd fucked up worse than before and was about to be killed by some blue-eyed twenty-three-year-old wearing sports gear.

Elliot approached, and Donnie pressed his teeth together until they hurt. He wasn't going to thrash around or call out. There was a cold inevitability to the moment, and the optimistic part of his mind told him at least he wouldn't have to face Yates the next day.

Elliot got closer, straddled Donnie, then lowered himself down into his lap. Donnie blinked in surprise. They were close together, and just as the idea of headbutting Elliot started to take form in Donnie's flagging mind, Elliot held the blade to his throat.

"Not gonna happen."

Elliot clutched at the back of Donnie's neck with his other hand, then slid his fingers up into his matted hair. Somehow it was more embarrassing feeling someone's fingers snag on the knots than looking at the mess in the mirror.

"The grunge look still in?"

"Go to hell."

"You'll meet me there too."

Donnie noticed how clear Elliot's skin looked, how clean he smelled, how bright his eyes shone, how full his lips were. The same way he catalogued Elliot, Elliot seemed to catalogue him.

"Long greasy hair, tatty old beard, dirty face, dozy-assed gaze. What the hell happened?"

Donnie exhaled sharply from his nose instead of answering.

"This 'Donnie King' is a has-been. Pathetic."

The knife still threatened Donnie's jugular, but Elliot's other hand held his face. Donnie could smell him—vanilla with a sprinkle of something spicy.

He looked back, and the cold inevitability and self-hatred came screeching to a halt.

"But the other one's in there somewhere, isn't he…"

Elliot moved his thumb against the uneven hair on Donnie's jaw, then stopped and looked deep into Donnie's eyes. The intense look Elliot gave him made him shiver.

"Do you know what else I heard about Donnie King?"

Donnie licked his lips, tasting blood. "What?"

"He fucks like a wild thing."

A thrill shot through Donnie at the words. He used to—he used to be just as ruthless and thorough at fucking, but the last time he tried, he'd got worn-out and given up eating ass. His lover was both unsatisfied and offended.

"Where did you hear that?" Donnie asked.

The way Elliot looked into his eyes and the weight of him on his lap were doing odd things to Donnie. His thighs were hot from where they touched the back of Elliot's. His nostrils pulsed with Elliot's scent, and his fast-darkening eyes were too good to look away from. Something stirred in Donnie, uncurling him from his tight ball of self-loathing.

He didn't know what the hell was happening, what was going on in Elliot's head. All he could do was wait to see what Elliot was going to do with him.

Donnie was at his mercy—at the bright-eyed twenty-three-year-old's mercy.

He'd fallen through yet another trapdoor.

Elliot leaned in slowly, gaze attached to Donnie's mouth, and brought their lips together. His were soft, and plump, and so hot they burned.

A sound of surprise left Donnie.

Donnie didn't kiss back, but his lips parted slightly of their own accord. Elliot's kiss was gentle, his hold on the Donnie's face even softer, and it drove him fucking crazy. Somehow soft and gentle, it made his heart go into overdrive, and his pulse frantically beat against the blade at his neck.

Being at Elliot's mercy and being kissed gently was both a turn-on and a massive humiliation. Forced into a kiss, aroused by it, it was a complete indignity, but he didn't hiss for Elliot to stop.

Donnie could feel the nicks, the sharp blade catching the skin, but he couldn't slow his heart down and didn't avoid the lips on his.

Elliot slipped his tongue past Donnie's sore lip into the warmth of his mouth. Wet, and smooth, and eager. The pendulum swung away from humiliation into arousal. Donnie's cock pressed painfully against his zipper. Everything felt too tight, too hard, and mortifyingly, too wet.

Donnie brushed his tongue against Elliot's, loving the feel of it. The taste of Elliot danced on his taste buds, despite the blood, despite the whiskey, Elliot tasted sweeter than any mouth Donnie had tasted before, and a forgotten longing filled him.

He wanted to own that mouth.

Donnie struggled against the restraints, wanting to touch, wanting to hold, and he knew the knife had cut him deeper when warmth flowed down his neck. Donnie dove his tongue inside Elliot's mouth like he needed the wetness and the heat. He sucked on Elliot's tongue, and he went all shaky on Donnie's lap, groaning into his mouth.

He didn't do gentle kisses, or soft touches, or let himself be led. He kissed and sucked and licked, and the other guy was supposed to get embarrassed over how much they wanted him. They surrendered, and Donnie did what he pleased until he was satisfied. That was the old Donnie's way.

He needed to establish order and kiss Elliot into submission. Donnie would be damned if he died while being teased with sweet kisses.

"Fuck," Elliot breathed, leaning back. "You may look a mess, but boy can you kiss a guy breathless."

He got up from Donnie's lap and took a step back. He dropped the knife, fondling his lips. Donnie could see they had blood on them—his blood—and his cock jolted in his pants.

"What now?"

"I leave."

"And me?"

Elliot rolled his eyes, smiling. He sauntered forward, then pressed a hand to Donnie's groin. He rubbed Donnie's cock until he grunted, then backed off.

"I leave you alive."

"You know I'll come after you," Donnie said, breathing heavily from his nose. "When I catch you, I will kill you."

"You'll never catch me, baby."

Donnie frowned. "What did you call me?"

Elliot's grin climbed higher, his eyes sparkled, and then he winked. "Baby."

"I dare you to say that again," Donnie growled.

"Bye, baby."

Elliot turned around, picked up the blue backpack, then left through the front door, leaving it open, exposing a tied-up Donnie to the corridor.

"Don't fucking call me baby!"

CHAPTER THREE

Donnie's shoulders ached, his head pounded, but he still trudged up the path to get to the flower shop. He wore the same jacket as the day before but had changed his bloodied T-shirt. The cuts on his neck were covered by a scarf, but he couldn't do anything to conceal the fat lip and the swollen cheek from where the frying pan had hit him.

He pushed open the door, and the bell dinged. Yates's deadly eyes met his for a second, before he went back to serving his customer.

His customer was dressed in a suit, holding a briefcase. There were roses on the counter, twelve massive red roses, and he shuffled foot to foot like he was desperate for a piss.

"I'm sure it'll be fine. Relax," Yates said, smiling.

A warm smile that was all fake, but the man with the briefcase didn't seem to notice. Yates looked like a good man dressed in his floral shirt, nodding encouragement and smiling.

Donnie knew different.

The man picked up the roses, bowed his head in thanks, then turned to leave.

He saw Donnie, stopped, then took a longer route around the shop to get to the door, keeping as much distance as he could.

"Don't worry, she's bound to say yes," Yates shouted.

The man turned around. "Thanks."

He passed through the door and hurried down the street.

"Get a room," Donnie mumbled.

The fake smile on Yates's face dropped. His expression could only be described as fierce, and Donnie wished the man he'd just sold flowers to came back and saw the real Yates.

"I'm taking you into a room—the back room—to strangle you."

"Hold on," Donnie said, lifting his hands in surrender.

"I told you what would happen if you fucked this up, and I thought you'd come to face it like a man. A part of me actually respected you for it, but here you are with your hands up, about to beg for another chance."

"He wasn't there."

Yates took a step back. "What?"

"He wasn't there. I waited outside the apartment, but he didn't show."

"Right, well, I've got his schedule. You can try again tonight."

"I broke into his apartment."

Yates narrowed his eyes and spoke through his teeth. "You did what?"

"Relax. I took out the camera, used the code, picked the lock, and left no trace."

"Really?"

Donnie rolled his eyes. "Yes, really. The point is, I couldn't find a passport or toothbrush. The drawers were open as if he'd packed a bag in a hurry. I think he's done a runner."

"Fuck," Yates said, smashing his fist down on the counter. "Took me months to find him."

"He's gone."

Yates frowned, eyeing Donnie's face. "What happened to you, then?"

"You really think that kid did this to me?"

"That's not what I said." Yates squinted at him. "I asked you what happened to your face."

"Oh. I tripped over—face-planted a door."

"You were drunk?"

"Guilty," Donnie said, but before Yates could launch at him, he quickly added, "I drank after I realized he wasn't there. No drink on the job."

"Good. I'll just have to find him again…"

"And when you find him?"

Yates glared across the shop at Donnie. "I'll tell you, and you finish the job…or else."

Donnie swallowed, backing away.

****

Somehow, he was still alive.

Yates had bought his lies, and Elliot—well, Elliot was a little asshole that in due course would regret not taking Donnie out when he had the chance.

If he hadn't had taken the bottle and drank half of it, the hit would've gone without a hitch. He glared at his traitorous minibar. The beers, the spirits, the whiskey—he itched to drink them, but had been holding back.

He ended up in a hot sweat on the sofa, panting his way through difficult dreams. He gasped at the explosion, the scrape of metal, the spit of fire. He sat up fast, clutching his chest. Only a dream, or more accurately a nightmare. He wiped his hand down his face and blinked back the sting in his eyes.

The front door boomed. Three distinct knocks, not of someone's fist, but of their boot as they kicked the bottom corner.

He heaved himself out of the groove in his sofa, then creeped as quietly as he could, soft on his toes like a jaguar. He leaned close to the peephole, and it took a few seconds for his eye to adjust. Ranger tilted his head the other side, glaring right into Donnie's eye.

"I know you're looking at me…"

Donnie snorted, unlocking the door. "How could you know?"

"I heard you stomp your way over to the door."

"I was quiet."

"No you weren't."

Ranger stepped into the room, then stopped with his hands on his hips.

"You look awful."

Donnie groaned. "I feel awful."

Ranger wore his black vest and black shades even though it was cold outside, but the most unique thing about Ranger was his hair—or head. Half of his head was shaved, showing off a scar he'd gotten tattooed into a snake.

He said he wanted brain surgery to look hot.

"Well, this is shit," Ranger said.

"This is my apartment."

"And it's gone to shit. What's with all the takeout bags and empty bottles."

Donnie looked around. There was garbage everywhere, and he hadn't cracked a window open in days.

"I've got a few full bottles too."

"You are thirty-five, not nineteen."

"I'm well aware of that."

"You got coffee? Decaf coffee? You know what I get like when I have caffeine."

"You practically bounce off the walls," Donnie said, walking into the kitchen. "It's instant."

"Considering this," Ranger said, jutting his chin out at the room, "I'm surprised you've even got that."

Donnie went about making them both coffees, while Ranger brushed away some of the packets and containers on the sofa so he could sit down. Donnie looked over to him. Two years ago Ranger would never have worn a tank top. Two years ago he wouldn't have even dropped by Donnie's apartment. Two years ago Ranger had been positively terrifying, more intense than Yates. He'd been a "dirty" assassin, hired to do the grubby jobs where limbs were hacked off and the blood flowed, but after his injury, Donnie decided not to tell him about his dark jobs, and Ranger completed simple hits to pay his lifestyle.

"So I hear you've got a job…" Ranger picked the photograph of Elliot off the coffee table. "This him?"

"Yeah, Elliot Austin."

"He's a hot one, isn't he."

Donnie looked away. "If you're into that."

"Blond, blue eyes, good body. Who isn't into that?" He paused, then looked over to Donnie. "I was into that before, right?"

"Yes, you weren't fussy over who you stuck your dick in as long as they took it and thanked you afterward."

Ranger put the photograph down. "That's a relief."

"You do know I'm gonna kill him, right?"

"I've killed one or two hot ones…probably more than that, but I can't remember. So you didn't get him last night?"

Donnie paused, then stirred a spoonful of sugar into his coffee. "No. He was already gone."

"Yeah, Yates told me earlier when I went in to see if he's got a job for me."

"Elliot was a no-show. Checked his apartment and looked like he'd done a runner."

"Huh…that's what Yates told me too, but I was bored, so thought I'd go check it out."

Donnie cursed under his breath.

He picked up both coffees and returned to his groove on the sofa. He handed Ranger his, then went to reach for the TV remote, but Ranger snatched it first. Some of his coffee spilled onto the back of his hand, but he didn't seem to feel it.

"I saw you sprayed the camera."

Donnie nodded. "Like I said."

"And the lock was still intact, but curiously scratched up pretty bad."

"It's not about the execution, it's about getting the job done."

Ranger shot Donnie one of his lopsided smiles. He'd never had that smile before, only a grimace. "And I spoke to Maggie."

"Who?"

"Maggie—nice lady, a nurse of all things. Lives in the apartment next to Elliot."

"Never heard of her."

Ranger tipped his head back laughing, spilling more coffee he didn't seem to feel. "She told me she came back from her shift and saw you from the corridor. Tied up?"

"Long hours these nurses work. She must've been tired."

"Relax, I'm not going to tell Yates."

Donnie narrowed his eyes. "Really?"

"Said so, didn't I... As long as you tell me what happened."

Donnie groaned. "That's almost as bad as telling Yates."

"Come on," Ranger said, "let's hear it."

"I took a bottle on the job."

"On second thoughts, maybe I will tell Yates..."

"I dropped it."

"Good."

"Elliot heard it, looked over. I didn't think he'd seen me."

"Then what happened?"

Donnie shrugged. "Waited till midnight, then sprayed the camera, got inside the building, and tried to pick the lock."

Ranger frowned. "What do you mean tried?"

"I couldn't do it. I thought I had, but Elliot opened the door. He smashed me in the face with a frying pan."

Ranger burst out laughing. He put his coffee on the table, but Donnie could see he'd spilled most of it on himself. Ranger didn't react to his red, raw hand. "No way. A frying pan?"

"I came to, tied to a chair."

"Was Elliot still there?"

Donnie decided he'd rather jump headfirst out the window than mention his and Elliot's conversation let alone the hot kiss.

"No, he'd gone."

"I think this one tops your last fuckup."

"Let's not mention that."

Ranger quirked his eyebrow. "No, let's."

"Ranger," Donnie growled.

"Hopefully I won't have to come to your rescue on this one too."

"You didn't come to my rescue."

"I cleaned up your botched job. The poor fucker was actually grateful I came to put him out of his misery. They're not supposed to look grateful."

"I thought he was dead."

"You shot him in the chest, somehow missing everything vital. He was bleeding for hours before I put him down." Ranger shook his head. "So unprofessional, and the time before that you missed completely, and he's still out there somewhere."

"I'm not gonna miss with this one."

"He took you out with a frying pan, then tied you up."

His voice lacked any emotion, and Donnie froze, wondering whether he was about to see the old Ranger, but instead he burst out laughing again.

Ranger never used to laugh.

"What?" Donnie said, narrowing his eyes.

"He tied you up, could've killed you but didn't. He must've thought you were that weak and easy he could leave you alive. How humiliating. You're a hit man, unworthy of being taken out by some kid you were sent to kill."

"Go to hell."

Ranger grabbed his coffee and took a sip. Donnie sipped his own, then winced when he burned his tongue.

"So what's the plan for him?"

"Yates is going to find him for me first, then I'll go in. I'll ditch the booze, have my head in the game, and take him out."

"Can I make a suggestion?"

"No. But you will anyway."

Ranger licked his lips. "Don't go in, stay out. Stay so far out he won't even see it coming."

"Huh?"

"He outsmarted you close up—"

"I wouldn't say that…"

"Kill him from long range. You used to be an incredible shot, or so I heard." Ranger tapped his head. "I can't actually remember."

Ranger had been the better shot when they practiced, and bragged endlessly about it, but that was before he took a bullet to the head. That wasn't the same Ranger sitting next to Donnie.

"I still am an incredible shot. You were always jealous of me."

"Yeah?"

Donnie hummed. "You'd beg for tips."

Ranger chuckled. "That settles it, then. You can borrow my rifle; I've got a new rear sight. Take him out from a distance with a messy head shot." Ranger kissed his fingers. "Beautiful."

"That could work."

Ranger smiled, then took another gulp of coffee. "Anyway, must dash. I'm on my way to a job."

"What job?"

He waved his hand dismissively, getting to his feet. "Got to take out some cheating husband."

"Any special requirements?"

"As it happens, yeah…"

Ranger reached into his pocket and pulled out a lacy red thong. "This has gotta be in his mouth while I strangle him." He stretched them out and held them over his crotch. "You think it suits me?"

"I don't want to picture you in lacy underwear."

"Fair enough," Ranger said, shoving them back in his pocket.

Donnie glanced back at his minibar. "Hey, Ranger, you wanna take some of my booze?"

Ranger scoffed. "Is the pope over sixty?"

"What?"

"Yes he is."

"I don't understand—"

"Yes, I want your booze. What can I have?"

"Everything."

"Everything?"

Donnie's heart pounded. He had to stop drinking, knew he did. He scrunched his eyes shut and shook his head. "Everything except the whiskey."

"You got it," Ranger said. "You got a bag?"

"Should be one in the kitchen on the side."

"Great."

Ranger gathered the bottles, knocking them together, and Donnie kept his eyes shut not to look. "I'll see you later, then, yeah?"

"Yeah."

Ranger went, and Donnie slowly turned to see behind him.

He hated the relief that filled him at seeing the whiskey still there.

CHAPTER FOUR

Yates gestured for Donnie to follow him into the back of the flower shop. He turned the sign on the door to closed, locked it, then hurried after him. It had been three weeks since his botched hit on Elliot Austin, and he needed to redeem himself.

"I found him."

Yates sat down at his desk, unlocked his drawer, and pulled out the huge folder on Elliot. "He didn't go too far."

"How did you find him?"

"I've got contacts around the city, put his face out, and his details, and struck gold. He's staying in the Fairview Hotel."

Donnie lifted his eyebrows. "Fairview? How the hell?"

Yates shrugged. "He's got money apparently. The hotel's got armed security, and he's in his room most of the time requesting room service, but he's fond of pancakes."

"Pancakes. Oh I see," Donnie said, nodding.

"What do you see?" Yates asked, tilting his head.

"Poison. I could lace them with poison."

"You could, or you could wait for him to leave the hotel and go to the pancake house across the street."

"That sounds better."

"I spoke to Ranger; he says he'll lend you his rifle."

"Yeah."

Yates glared at him. "When was the last time you practiced?"

Months...a year.

"More recently than you think."

"I will kill you if you fuck this up, again."

"I didn't fuck it up the first time. He wasn't there."

Yates huffed, then opened the folder. "I've done you the courtesy of marking up a map."

Donnie leaned over the table, taking it in.

"Pancake house is opposite the hotel. You're not going to get a vantage point there. I suggest here." Yates pressed his forefinger down on the map. "Get on the roof. You'll be five floors up, the angle will be tight, but it's doable. If you can't get him sitting at his table, then get him when he walks across the road. You used to be good at moving targets."

"I still am good."

"Then this won't be a problem, then, will it."

"No problem."

"I've marked up the area for cameras. There's a police station five miles away. The key is to be quick. See him, shoot him, then go."

"I'm not exactly gonna wait around to be caught, am I…"

Yates looked at him seriously. "With you, Donnie, I don't know anymore. He leaves the hotel each morning for the pancake house."

"He's got a sweet tooth," Donnie muttered.

He clacked his tongue to the roof of his mouth, remembering the kiss, the taste, the humiliation of the whole meeting.

"I don't know what kind of 'tooth' he has; I just want you to stop them chewing, right?"

"Right."

Yates handed him the map, then raised his eyebrow when Donnie didn't leave.

"You wanna kiss my feet again?"

"What—no."

"Then get out."

Donnie bit his lip, then asked, "Who's taken the hit out on him?"

Yates's eyebrows met in the middle. "Why?"

"I wanna know, that's all."

"Marco Russo."

Donnie nodded. "I've done hits for him before."

"Yeah, back when you were good—"

"I'm still good."

"He used you a few times—he quite liked you and your reputation back then, but news travels fast when you fuck up. Hanson Sale is still out there somewhere after all."

Donnie huffed. "The second he comes out of hiding, I'm on it. He's the first—the only man I couldn't kill."

"Only needs one to ruin your reputation, and it's only because of Ranger it's one fuckup and not two." Yates waved his hand. "Maybe you can claw back some of your reputation if you kill this kid."

"Why does Marco want him dead?"

"He stole a load of drug money from him apparently."

"How much?"

"A sizeable amount if Marco wants him dead. Now enough with the questions. Get out of my shop, and kill Elliot Austin."

Donnie saluted. "Yes, sir."

"And don't do that." Yates snorted.

"What?"

"Salute me. It's getting me hard, and I doubt you want to be bent over my desk. The longer you stay there, the bigger the possibility is of that happening, and right now, we both know you're not strong enough to stop me spreading your legs…"

Donnie lowered his hand, then backed out of the room. "No, thanks."

****

His vantage point was at least 650 feet from the pancake house. He was dressed all in black, had a huge sports bag with Ranger's gun inside. He watched the street below with binoculars. They trembled slightly in his grip despite him not drinking that morning. He'd managed to beat back his cravings for the kill, but once he was back at his apartment, he would celebrate and drink a whole bottle.

He was five stories up but still vulnerable to being spotted from the towering hotel.

The Fairview Hotel was fit for royalty. A single night cost thousands of dollars. Elliot didn't seem shy about spending his stolen wealth; he flaunted it. Most people went to ground after they realized a hit was out on them, but not Elliot.

Elliot did the equivalent of peacocking.

Once Donnie recovered from the walk up the five flights of stairs, he went back to waiting. The tortuously slow wait where his mind threw up his failures. He was half concentrating on the people walking below, half reliving his personal nightmares.

Hanson Sale had slipped through his grasp. It was all lined up to be an easy hit, but Donnie had missed his shots—not one, but all five in the clip. He'd gone for his knife to finish Hanson instead, but a mixture of alcohol in his system, fatigue, and second-guessing had him messing that up too, or so he supposed.

He'd woken up two hours later to a confused taxi driver, but the point was, Hanson had gotten away and gone to ground.

Hanson had been clever, but Elliot hadn't been.

It was about to cost him dearly.

The bitter wind brushed his neck, and Donnie shivered. Yates had planned for everything except the weather. Donnie knew he'd have to adjust his shot, get it just right with the air blasting him in odd intervals. His long hair whipped across his face, tickling under his nostrils and snagging on his unordered beard. The pancake house opened at seven, and according to Yates's intelligence, Elliot went out early.

A few people crossed the road to get to the pancake house. Donnie tracked them through his binoculars, hoping to see a familiar blond mop of hair. When he finally did, he gasped, craning his neck forward as if it somehow helped.

Donnie saw Elliot cross the street. He could only see the back of him but knew it was him from the size, the swagger, his messy blond hair, and narrow waist. The confidence was astounding. He wasn't rushing across the road or walking in a half crouch. He strolled with his head high, and Donnie couldn't wait to put a bullet through it.

Elliot passed into the pancake shop, and Donnie got ready. He could see the tables, could see Elliot in the queue, but the angle was all wrong. He didn't want to hit someone else by accident. He wanted a clean shot—clean in execution, not in what it left behind.

Elliot ordered, then went over to the table by the window. Donnie smiled; the assassination gods were finally showering him with some luck. The wind blasted him from the right, but he kept steady, kept his eyes on his mark.

Elliot put something on the table, what looked like a notebook. He twirled a pen in his fingers and frowned at the book. Donnie couldn't wait to splatter that blank page red.

Elliot chewed on his lip, his plump pink lip. Donnie found himself doing the same. His own were dry from the wind, cracked, rough, but Elliot's looked soft—hell, they were soft.

Donnie could still remember. Why was he remembering when he was about to blow his brains out?

Elliot looked out the window and rested his chin on his hand, pondering. Donnie placed the binoculars on the floors and unzipped the bag. He lifted his lips in a savage smile when he saw the gun—powerful, vicious, efficient. Assassins like him needed to be a good shot, the best. A strike worthy of a snake.

This was it. Donnie was going to redeem himself and punish Elliot for his overconfidence, and that humiliating kiss.

The safety was off. Donnie's usually tremoring hands went deadly still with his grip on the gun. He got in position, found Elliot through the sight.

He took a deep breath, forefinger ready for the shot.

The wind blew at him again, not enough to move him in his poised state. He'd locked on Elliot and locked down his body, immovable, impenetrable, all except for his unkempt hair that struck him in the face—his eye to be exact. The stray strand caught him like razor wire, and he blinked as he pulled sharply on the trigger.

The shot rang out, and the loud metallic clank shouted out triumph, but when Donnie looked down the sight, his guts flopped out of his body onto the ground, and a gasp caught in his throat.

He'd missed.

He watched the circular scene unfold in slow motion. The man beside Elliot with the chunk missing from his head. His slow fall to the ground, the microsecond where no one reacted, before everyone in the pancake house threw themselves down.

Donnie prepared to fire again, but not only did Elliot have cover from the table, but from the front wall of the café too. He couldn't see him, and firing off shot after shot was unlikely to get him a result, just a more damning failure.

There were shouts, a few screams, but Donnie stayed completely still in the chance Elliot would make a mistake—run from the pancake house or stand up for a second. Donnie watched his table, and his heart jumped into his throat when he saw movement.

He could still do it; he could still redeem himself.

Something slid up, something sprayed in blood.

Elliot's sketch pad—not notebook—creeped up over the top of the table. It was peppered in a spray of blood, but Donnie could still see what Elliot had written on it.

Baby?

The rage bubbled up in his veins. The arrogant, bold little shit had called him baby, again. Against the warning in his head, he fired another shot, hitting home through the a on Baby. The notepad disappeared. Donnie breathed hard and fast through his nose. He had to get out of there and fast. The anger consumed him, filling his face with heat.

Elliot was mocking him, humiliating him…again.

Donnie could hear sirens, could see people at their windows in the hotel next to him. He took one last look through the sight, meaning it only to be a glance, but he froze when he saw the pad of paper again, flapping to get his attention.

Elliot had scribbled out the question mark and added a word above baby.

Bye, Baby.

"You little shit," Donnie hissed.

Part of him wanted to go to the pancake house and strangle Elliot to death in front of everyone, getting caught be damned, but he was a professional—not a very good professional from his last two tries, but he was still one.

Donnie abandoned his position, and his chance of redeeming himself, and ran for the exit. Back down the flights of stairs that had nearly killed him on the ascent, he ran down the side of the building, through the carefully mapped-out getaway Yates had provided.

Yates hadn't planned for him being so slow at reacting. Yates hadn't planned for his flagging fitness. The sirens were right behind him, and the blue lights reflected off the windows he rushed past. The blond with the blue eyes and the soft lips and the overconfidence was his ultimate downfall.

Donnie was done for, except someone was waiting for him at the end of the alley.

Someone on a bike, wearing a balaclava. Ranger was wearing another tank top, tight-fitting jeans, and his boots. He revved the bike, a clear sign he wanted Donnie to hurry the hell up. Donnie rasped and spluttered but managed to get to him. He jumped on the back of the bike, sandwiching the sports bag between Ranger's back and his front.

"Go!"

Ranger took off down the alley, out onto the road. He dodged traffic like a pro—didn't care about mounting the curb or driving through a shopping mall. Donnie gritted his teeth, certain they were gonna crash. That, or die in a collision with a man on a mobility scooter.

"You see that?" Ranger shouted.

"What?"

"That dude cut me off."

Ranger turned sharply, looping around seating and an escalator in the middle of the mall.

"What the hell are you doing!"

Ranger rode back the way they'd come, and people dived out the way, scurrying to hide from the bike. Donnie spied the man on the mobility scooter over Ranger's shoulder.

"Don't kill him!"

"Who said I was gonna kill him?"

He rode straight up to the man and stopped, wagging his finger, and in the same voice people told off their dogs said, "No."

The man's lips popped open, and he looked around for help. "What?"

"What you did back there. No. I had right of way, I shouldn't have had to swerve."

"I'm sorry."

"Apology accepted."

Donnie shook Ranger's shoulder. "Let's get the hell out of here."

"I'm on it."

Chapter Five

Yates stood behind the counter of the flower shop, nostrils pulsing, eyes unwavering in their focus. The one time Donnie wanted there to be a customer, there wasn't one. His brain screamed at him to turn around and run the fuck away, but he knew Yates would follow. Yates would find him and give him a slow death rather than a quick one.

"Come into the back."

Donnie shook his head. "No, you gotta hear me out first."

"Lower the blinds and I will."

An uncomfortable laugh escaped Donnie. "Nah, I'm not falling for that."

"You missed."

He couldn't deny he'd missed. It was all over the news. He hadn't known it at the time, but the man he'd taken out owned the pancake house. Simon Gear. Donnie had covered most of the customers in a spray of Simon's blood.

"Not only did you miss, but you hit someone else, and now I've gotta hope your incompetence doesn't lead back to me."

"It was the wind."

"Well, you're gonna feel mighty draughty when I've put holes through you."

"Come on, Yates—"

"Don't 'come on' me! I gave you an easy hit—my easy hit—and you messed it up."

"It wasn't my fault; it was the wind…and…and…"

"And what?"

Donnie tapped his head. "That fucker with the massive forehead. He got in the way."

The bell to the flower shop dinged. Donnie inwardly prayed the old lady or the engagement guy had walked in behind him.

"What's happening, bitches?"

Donnie didn't think it was possible, but Yates looked even angrier after the greeting from Ranger. Ranger pushed his shades up into his hair and grinned at them both.

"I've only got enough space in here for one idiot at a time," Yates muttered.

"If that was the case, no one would ever come in."

Yates narrowed his eyes. "Why are you here?"

"To stop you killing Donnie."

Donnie turned to him. "Thank you."

"If anyone deserves to kill him, it's me."

"Woah. Hold on," Donnie said, distancing himself from Ranger. "What the hell?"

"You were nearly caught. I would've lost my gun, and I had to be your getaway, so you kinda owe me."

"I only missed because of the wind—the wind. Can you really kill a man over wind?"

Yates stayed stone-faced, but Ranger burst out laughing.

"Yes, I can," Yates answered. "Ranger, lower the blinds."

Ranger's laughter stopped abruptly. He shot a pitying smile at Donnie, and twiddled the blinds until they fell like a guillotine.

"One more chance," Donnie said.

Yates came out from behind the counter, cracking his knuckles.

"You want me to beg, I'll beg."

"Go on, then."

Donnie flashed looks back and forth between Yates and Ranger before dropping to his knees. "One more chance at killing him, please."

He raised his hands in a prayer pose, full-on begging.

"Come on, Yates."

"Say I'm the sexiest man you've ever seen."

Donnie flexed his face. The words were poison in his mouth, but he still forced them out. "You're the sexiest man I've ever seen."

"Tell me how badly you wanna suck my cock."

"What?"

"Go on. Make it convincing."

"No—"

"You want to live, don't you?"

"I really wanna suck your cock," Donnie said through his teeth.

Yates looked at Ranger. "Did that convince you?"

"Nope."

"Right, then," Yates said, "I'll get my gun."

"I want to suck your cock. I want to run my hands up and down it and lap at your balls like a dog."

Yates hummed. "And what noises will you make while you do it?"

"I'll tell you how good you taste, how big you are."

"I'm not into sex talk."

Donnie swallowed. "Then I'd whimper and whine like a hungry dog. A dog desperate for praise from its master."

"Who wants to know he's been a good boy," Yates said, nodding. "That's a good image right there."

"Yeah. I'll whimper like that."

Ranger forcefully cleared his throat.

"What?" Yates snapped.

"You're hard right now."

"Of course I'm hard. A whimpering mutt is a good look on Donnie."

Ranger scrunched his forehead. "He looks pathetic."

"I have a kink for pathetic men."

"Good to know. It's not for me…or at least I don't think it is—was—you know what I mean," Ranger said, dusting his hands together. He looked around the shop, and picked out a rose and took a deep inhale. Yates tore his heated gaze off Donnie and attached it to Ranger getting high on a rose. He kept sniffing, and Donnie watched as Yates's tented pants went down.

"Don't do that."

"What?"

"Sniff my flower."

"Your flower…gross, for some reason I'm picturing your asshole. Not a place I'd wanna sniff."

The skin around Yates's nose tightened as he snarled, "Keep pissing me off and I won't give you a choice."

"I only sniffed a goddamn flower. That's what you're supposed to do."

"If you're going to buy them, yes, but you're not, are you."

Ranger shrugged. "Maybe I was, but I'm not gonna now."

"You're so full of shit."

"Isn't everyone?"

"Don't touch the flowers, understand?"

"Why you getting all weird about it. This shop is a cover—"

"It's my shop. My flowers. My hard work."

"Hey," Donnie shouted, making a time-out sign with his hands. "So are we doing this?"

"It's not like you've got somewhere to be," Yates said.

"I'd rather be spared your petty argument."

Yates sighed. "Okay then."

Donnie squeezed his eyes shut. He heard Yates approach, his slow plods of doom across the shop floor. Donnie sensed Yates had stopped in front of him, his shoes pressed against Donnie's knees.

He jerked when Yates patted him on the head, then slowly opened his eyes.

"Good dog."

Donnie licked his lips. "What?"

"I'm not gonna kill you."

"But I missed the shot?"

Yates frowned. "I thought it was the wind?"

"Yeah, it was—"

"Simon Gear. Owner of the pancake house. Also the owner of hundreds of indecent pictures of children. He won't be missed. If you'd have hit anyone else though, there'd be a bullet going through your forehead right now."

Donnie exhaled slowly. "I've got another chance?"

"Yes. But I want sixty percent."

"What?" Donnie shouted, getting to his feet.

Yates squared up against him, wider, taller, stronger. Donnie didn't have a chance if it came to blows.

"It's me that has to find him…again."

"Fine," Donnie mumbled.

"Now both of you get the hell out of my shop."

Ranger shoved his nose in the rose one last time, then put it back in the vase. He followed Donnie out of the shop, but Donnie had no desire to walk with him. He planned to go home, wallow in self-pity, and drink whiskey until he was unconscious.

"Hold up," Ranger said.

"How about no…"

"Who's twisted your balls?"

"No one."

"Is that the problem?"

Donnie sighed, glancing at Ranger. "Thanks for saving my ass."

"I said I wanted to shoot it—"

"I didn't mean just then, but yesterday."

Ranger chuckled. "I knew you'd mess it up."

"How?"

"Gut feeling. So what happened?"

"The wind."

"It wasn't that strong, a few gusts, but—"

Donnie shook his head. "It blew my hair into my eye."

"Right…"

"Lame, I know, but that's what happened."

Ranger rubbed his hands together. "Well, we know what you've gotta do."

"Kill Elliot as quickly as possible."

"Yes, but I didn't mean that. I meant it's time you get your hair cut."

"My hair's fine."

"It looks like someone dumped a load of egg whites on it."

"Thanks for the feedback."

"As I see it, you owe me. And I'm kinda fed up of looking at that mess…"

Donnie sighed. "Do I have a choice in this?"

"Yeah, there's a choice. You either get your hair done, or you go home and drink yourself into oblivion."

"Clearly gonna choose the latter."

"But if you do that, I'll break into your apartment while you're asleep and shave all your hair off—actually, I'll shave one line down the center of your head."

"You wouldn't."

Ranger lifted his chin, grinning. "I so would."

"Fine. I'll get it cut."

"Great. There's a good place over there," Ranger said, pointing.

Calvin Cuts. A small barber's shop on the corner of the street. Ranger ushered Donnie toward the door, then shoved him inside.

"We need some serious hair care, Calvin."

Calvin turned around, and the first thing Donnie noticed was his long beard, black as night and in much better condition than Donnie's ratty facial hair. Calvin had a long moustache which curled at the ends, and the thickest pair of black eyebrows Donnie had ever seen.

Calvin took one look at Donnie's hair, then dragged him by the hand over to the sink.

He sat awkwardly on the chair, with his legs splayed out and his neck bent back into the basin in the most uncomfortable position known to man.

"You know, I heard you can get strokes from those sinks," Ranger said.

"You're telling me this now."

Ranger shrugged. "I thought you'd wanna know."

"Well, I didn't."

Calvin leaned over him. "Before I can do anything, I've got to wash it…several times."

He turned on the showerhead, testing it on his hand before wetting down Donnie's hair. He rubbed in shampoo, and conditioner, and his skilled hands on Donnie's scalp made up for his neck ache.

Calvin took the rinse and repeat instructions to the maximum, and when he finally released Donnie's neck, it felt weaker, like it couldn't support his head. He moved to the chair and shook his hair, spraying Ranger head to toe in droplets.

"You really are a dog."

"So what are we doing today?" Calvin asked.

Before Donnie had even opened his mouth, Ranger had pointed to a hair model on the wall. "That."

"Good choice."

"Do I get a say?" Donnie asked.

Ranger got up and grabbed a magazine from the rack. "No say. Now shut up and let Calvin work his magic."

Donnie stared at the table in front of the mirror rather than himself. He'd avoided his reflection as much as he could. There was a time he'd check himself out in shop windows, in car side mirrors, in dog tags if they greeted him in the street.

But that had been before he messed up. He'd been able to look at himself then; he'd actually cared what he looked like and how others saw him, but over the last year he'd actively avoided looking at his face.

When he grew tired of staring at the table, he lowered his gaze to the floor. He could see his clumped strands of wet hair everywhere. He hadn't realized it had gotten so long until it was scattered over the floor like hay for a horse.

"And can you do something about the beard?" Ranger said.

Calvin nodded. "Sure thing."

"Shape it, trim it a bit, maybe dye the gray hairs."

"Hey," Donnie said. "I don't have any gray hairs."

"You have a few," Calvin said, "but I'm on it."

Donnie went back to staring at the floor. The shaver buzzed, scissors snipped, and Ranger turned the pages of his magazine. Donnie concentrated on the noise, and his eyes slid shut. Elliot hid behind his eyelids, his cocky grin, his burning blue eyes… and then Donnie's ears buzzed with the most irritating sound of all.

Elliot's teasing voice calling him baby.

"Hey!"

Donnie opened his eyes and found Calvin's in the mirror. "What is it?"

"You trying to break your teeth or something? You're grinding them hard."

"Sorry…"

Calvin tilted Donnie's head and started on his tattered beard.

"I'm gonna trim it right down. Stylish stubble."

Donnie went back to watching his hair fall to the floor. He didn't know how long it took, but Ranger got up a few times to get a different magazine.

"Have you written into this one?"

"What are you talking about?"

"Listen to this: I'm stuck in a rut and end up drinking a bottle of whiskey each night."

"Are you reading the problem page?"

"Yep. Wanna know the advice?"

Donnie sighed. "No. But you're gonna tell me anyway."

"It says you've taken the first step and recognized you've got a problem."

"I haven't got a problem."

"Seek help, and don't bottle up your emotions."

"Poor choice of words…"

"Open up to loved ones."

Donnie snorted. "You and Yates are my closest friends, and you almost came to blows over who would kill me."

Calvin paused, then shook his head.

"Doesn't mean we don't love you," Ranger said.

Donnie rolled his eyes.

"I'm desperate to date, but my job always gets in the way. Will I ever find the one?"

"Well, that's not me."

"No," Ranger sighed. "It's me though."

Donnie laughed. "Good one."

Ranger didn't say anything back, and after a few minutes the silence grew too uncomfortable to bear. Donnie recoiled at Ranger's hurt expression.

"I'm not joking."

"You're being serious?"

"Yes, I'm being serious."

"Well...okay then..."

Ranger continued to watch him through the mirror with his wounded expression.

"It's just..." Donnie started.

"Just what?"

"You always hated being tied down. Said you couldn't stand baggage."

Ranger looked down at the floor. "That's not how I feel now. Being tied down sounds pretty fucking great actually, and I don't mean the way Yates likes to do it, but having an anchor, a connection to someone else, always there."

"And baggage?"

"Why is baggage bad? I'd love baggage. Someone to pick up and take home, to unzip, to unpack all the bad and stuff in all the good. Someone that could be mine, exclusively mine. Who wouldn't want baggage?"

Donnie moved his gaze away from Ranger and looked at Calvin. Calvin pressed his lips together hard and bobbed his head. "Kinda nice, your friend, isn't he?"

"He's barking mad."

Calvin turned to Ranger. "Why not try online dating?"

Donnie snorted. "What the hell would he put as his job title?"

"What do you do?"

"I kill people," Ranger said, grinning.

Donnie parted his lips, about to spew out a hundred denials, but Calvin shook his head, laughed, then went back to Donnie's jawline.

"Good sense of humor. That's what you should put on your profile... We're about done."

"And you have done a top job," Ranger said.

"What do you think?" Calvin asked.

Donnie took a deep breath, and forced his gaze on himself. He focused on his hair, not his dead eyes, and he gawped. Shorter on the sides, longer on the top with a slight wave to it. His beard was smartly trimmed, his sideburns shaped. He looked good—or at least his hair did.

Donnie tentatively raised his hand and touched the side of his head, the spiky hairs where it was cut short. He leaned forward, and the longer hair on top shined with health, not grease. It was soft, smooth, back to chestnut brown instead of the grungy color his lack of care had turned it.

"Thank you," he whispered.

Calvin smiled. "No problem. The difference it makes—hotter, younger, friendlier."

"I wouldn't go that far," Donnie muttered.

"Make sure you spread the word in the community."

Donnie scrunched his face. "Community? What do you mean?"

"The homeless? Free cuts for the homeless."

Ranger's chuckle gathered momentum until he barked a laugh, slapping the magazine down on his thigh.

"What's his problem?"

"Nothing," Donnie said. "I'll spread the word, don't worry."

"Anything to help."

"You're a good man."

Donnie struggled out of the sheet around him, and handed it to Calvin.

"Thanks again," he said, before grabbing Ranger's arm and leading him from the shop.

"I got a haircut. You satisfied?"

"It looks good!"

Donnie resisted the urge to check himself out in a car window.

"But I'm not done with you yet."

"Where we going now?"

Ranger flicked his chin out toward his car. "Firing range."

"Firing range?"

"Yep. We're gonna start going again, three times a week, get you shooting good. Can't have this kid humiliating you anymore. Next time you get a chance, bullet between his eyes."

His burning blue eyes.

Donnie rubbed his temple, nodding. "Good idea."

CHAPTER SIX

Donnie breathed deep, exhaled slowly, and pulled the trigger, not once, but five times. The bullets sailed through the air, all missing the bull's-eye target on the chest and instead passing through the head of the silhouette printed on the paper.

Five neat holes.

Ranger punched his shoulder, and Donnie smiled, slipping his ear protectors off. Despite it being dark inside the room, Ranger continued to wear his shades. It didn't affect his shot; he'd been blowing paper brains out of the targets since they'd started.

"Perfect, buddy. Just think three weeks ago you missed nearly every shot."

"I wasn't that bad."

"You were, but you've got better. That's the important thing."

Donnie smiled. "Who would've thought you'd be helping me."

Ranger frowned. "What would I have been doing?"

"The old you would've stood behind me with his arms crossed, shaking his head in disapproval, telling me there was no hope and I should give up."

"Really?"

"Then you probably would've shot me in the kneecaps."

"The old me sounds like a dick."

"He wasn't... Different, that's all."

"He certainly wouldn't have got you a present, would he?"

"No, I can safely say you've never got me a present."

Ranger wagged his finger. "But the new Ranger has."

He walked away and came back again with a cardboard tube. Donnie had asked about it when they came in, but Ranger had told him to wait and see.

"What is it?"

Ranger grinned, opening the tube. He pulled the poster out, then rolled it for himself to see before turning it to Donnie.

"It's your blue-eyed blond."

Donnie stared at the huge picture of Elliot. The same picture Yates had. Elliot beaming at the camera—coy smile, and a glimpse of flesh right down his middle to his belly button.

Donnie looked away.

"You not like it?"

"I..."

"Well, you're not supposed to. You're supposed to put holes in it. I'll set it up."

Donnie scratched the back of his head as he watched Ranger change the target to Elliot. He didn't know why his cheeks burned. He hadn't been expecting to see Elliot like that.

Elliot looking good.

Donnie shook his head. Elliot was a little shit that needed to die, not just because he was Donnie's target, but because he'd tied him up, kissed him, and taunted him from under a table.

He needed to die.

"All set."

Donnie reloaded the clip, slamming it in hard. He slipped the ear protectors back down, and waited for Ranger to do the same. Ranger gave him a thumbs-up, then looked at the target.

Donnie's hands were shaking. They hadn't shaken for weeks, but they were trembling as rage filled his body. Elliot had smashed him around the face with a frying pan. Elliot had dragged him into a chair and tied him up. Elliot had climbed onto his lap and parted his lips with his tongue.

Elliot had got him humiliatingly hard.

Donnie fired, all five bullets one after the other.

All of them missed, hitting around Elliot's face rather than penetrating through. Donnie lowered the gun, and his head, and ended up staring wide-eyed at the table in front of him.

Ranger tapped his shoulder.

"What?" Donnie asked, before slipping his ear protectors off.

"It should be me asking what...as in, what the hell happened?"

Donnie shook his head. "I don't know."

"I'll tell you what happened—"

"I missed," Donnie said, pointing at Elliot's smug face.

His smug, attractive face.

"You got angry."

"What?"

"You got all red in the cheeks, your hand was shaking, you looked furious, like you wanted him dead."

"I do want him dead."

"You looked like it was personal."

"It is—"

"No it's not. It's a job, a hit. It's not supposed to be personal. You're not supposed to be angry. He's a nobody you've got to kill for cash. Elliot Austin isn't your enemy."

"Ranger is right."

Donnie jumped at the sound of Yates's voice but didn't turn around to look at him.

"How long you been there?"

"Elliot isn't your enemy. You are."

"Well, that's some psychological crap right there…"

"You've been all over the place since—"

Donnie raised his hand, and Yates didn't carry on. He didn't need to. They all knew why Donnie had slipped. Even Ranger recovering from brain surgery at the time knew what happened.

"So why are you here?"

Yates sighed. "Someone called me. They've found Elliot."

Donnie turned around. "Where?"

"He's been spotted in Key City. Mill Lane Shopping Mall, living it up apparently."

"How long ago?"

"I got the call forty-five minutes ago. If you hurry, he might still be around the area."

Yates stepped forward and snatched the gun from Donnie's hand. "Lay off the firearms for now. Get in close, stab him. It's not difficult."

"A stab and go," Ranger said, grinning.

Donnie nodded.

He turned back to the picture of Elliot. "I'm coming for you."

****

Donnie knew it would be like finding a needle in a haystack, but he hoped Elliot was still foolish enough to stand out in a crowd. Donnie walked through the shopping mall, looking in each window to get a glimpse of Elliot's messy, blond hair. He prowled the place, back and forth, and grew more and more disheartened.

He got his phone out to text Yates, but then he saw him.

Short blond hair, confident swagger, and a shirt that couldn't have been deemed more peacocking if he tried. It was literally a hideous peacock-print shirt. He held several bags, all expensive brands, and acted like he didn't have a care in the world.

The knives in Donnie's pocket tripled in weight, calling out to him. He had another chance, he just had to get close enough. Donnie followed Elliot at a distance at first. The Saturday crowds slowed his progress, but he managed to get closer, slipping behind Elliot.

Two people were between them, and Elliot hadn't changed his behavior.

Elliot turned his head, looked at a shop, then froze.

Donnie stopped too and followed Elliot's gaze to the shop. The shop with the huge glass window, acting like a mirror, reflecting them. Donnie tried to find something to duck behind, but there was nothing, only more people who were all shorter, frowning at him for stopping in the middle of the crowd. Elliot slowly turned his head back to face the way he was walking, then dropped his bags. He took off in a sprint, and Donnie ran after him.

Assassins needed to be fit and quick. As fast as a cheetah, as ferocious as a tiger, not a fat cat that enjoyed sitting in front of the fireplace.

Donnie knew he was out of shape; he'd seen his body slowly change over time, had gotten more and more exhausted doing the simplest things, like walking the flights of stairs to his apartment.

He used to run at them no problem, a skip in his step, but recently he'd started gripping the banister and half dragging himself up. He always got to his door panting and desperate for a drink. He should've drunk water but always found himself reaching for the whiskey bottle once he staggered through the door.

The crowds helped at least, slowing Elliot, all until he went the wrong way up an escalator. Donnie ran after him and then began the most humiliating moment of his life. He ran on the spot, unable to make any progress up the moving stairs. He didn't want to admit defeat, not when he had an audience, but he couldn't run fast enough. Embarrassment flooded his cheeks, and his thighs burned from effort, but still his pride demanded he keep going.

Elliot stopped at the top and looked over the edge, laughing. More people joined in the laughing, pointing at Donnie huffing and heaving on the bottom two steps of the escalator.

He gave up and looked across the mall.

There was an elevator, and he rushed over to it, determined to catch Elliot on the floor above. He hadn't moved from where he'd stood laughing, and just as Donnie got close, he grabbed the edge of the barrier and heaved himself over. Donnie's breath caught in his throat when he saw him drop, but Elliot had clung on to the side of the escalator before dropping to the ground.

Donnie looked over, and Elliot looked up at him. He smiled at Donnie, and bowed.

There were people clapping Elliot, actually clapping him.

"Little shit," Donnie hissed before trudging back to the elevator.

Elliot waited for him on the ground floor and gestured at Donnie to chase him. He started running again despite his legs cramping and the need to vomit rising. They ran through the mall, Donnie puffing and panting, while Elliot laughed like a kid. He kept stopping and looking at his watch, or yawning, or leaning on the wall waiting for him to catch up. It all added to the humiliation boiling Donnie alive.

They ran outside, and Donnie's jaw dropped as he watched Elliot. The kid was practically flying, leaping downstairs, hauling himself over walls, jumping from pillar to pillar. He had a gift for movement and flipped and leapt and defied the laws of physics. At one point he ran up a wall and had enough momentum to grab the railing above.

Donnie ran up the steps, puffing and heaving. His sides burned, and his lungs screamed out in protest, but he kept pushing. Elliot headed up the fire escape to the roof of a spa, trapping himself. All Donnie had to do was follow, then cut off his exit.

Donnie was yet again mistaken when they got to the roof. Elliot smiled, lifted his eyebrow, then ran to the edge. He leapt, cleared it, and landed with a roll on the other side.

The gap between the buildings had to be at least twenty feet wide. Maybe it would've been doable when he was in his prime, but Donnie shook his head, denying it physically as well as mentally.

He couldn't follow.

Elliot had gotten away.

Donnie dropped to his knees, then collapsed even further, supporting himself on his forearms. He gasped for breath while black spots danced in his vision. He internally chanted at himself not to be sick, to hold it in. He could taste the bile at the back of his mouth. It burned the delicate flesh of his throat. His heart was drumming in his chest, punching so hard he could feel his blood moving around his body, feel each pulse point throbbing against his skin.

Donnie breathed slow and deep, over and over.

He didn't know how much time had passed, but eventually his heart stopped beating manically, and his lungs stopped twisting into knots. They detangled and he savored a breath. Every muscle in his body ached, but he'd fought off the cardiac arrest.

Donnie froze at thud and huff to his right. He scrunched his eyes shut, wishing Elliot away.

"Breathe, baby."

Donnie turned his head and gritted his teeth. "Don't call me baby."

"That was some run we did back there."

"Enough…go."

"Is that all you got?"

"Evidently, yes."

"Pathetic."

Donnie flared his nostrils. "Go away."

Elliot hummed. "I can't go until I know you're gonna be all right."

"Fuck you."

"That's not very nice."

"I'll only be all right when you're dead."

"And who knows when that'll be?" Elliot shrugged, moving away. He peered down at the road. "You didn't want to try to jump it?"

"That would be stupid, wouldn't it."

"And so was trying to run the wrong way up the escalator, but you did it…"

Donnie groaned. He wanted to block that memory out as quickly as possible.

"And it was one of the funniest things I've ever seen, so thank you for that."

"Just…" he started.

"Just what?"

Donnie wanted to launch after Elliot, but knew Elliot would only skip out the way, humiliate him some more. He was done, utterly drained, and defeated by a man wearing a peacock-print shirt.

"Leave me alone."

God, he did sound utterly pathetic, but he wanted Elliot gone.

Elliot circled him. "It was you that ran after me."

"I've stopped, so you can go away now."

"Nah, I'm good. I like looking down on you. Makes me feel all high-and-mighty."

Donnie had never wanted someone to die that badly in his life. Elliot walked around him again, and Donnie moved his head, trying to keep him in his sights the whole time.

"You're an annoying fly."

"And you're the dead carcass I'm buzzing around."

"Why don't you go and fall off this building."

Elliot laughed. "Why don't you get off your lazy ass and push me."

"Not my style."

"As if that's the reason."

Donnie pushed off from his forearms and collapsed back. He sat on his ass, with his hands on the roof, propping himself up. His thighs were burning, and he looked at them as if he could see scorch marks through his pants. Elliot stood close, but not close enough to grab. He tilted his head, studying Donnie intently.

"What?"

"I'm digging the hair. You look like a million bucks, baby."

Donnie put venom into his glare.

Elliot smiled, rocking forward on his feet. "A million bucks that was rolled through dog shit."

"You've got a dirty little mouth on you."

"You've got no idea how dirty my mouth can get. I'd love you to get my mouth all dirty, filthy, and sticky."

"I will when I kill you and your blood runs out of it."

Elliot fondled his pink bottom lip. "Would the blood run over down here?"

Donnie heard his lip pop, and Elliot grinned, then ran his finger down his chin, slowly, opening his mouth as he did. His eyelashes fluttered, and he whined sharply. All the blood filling Donnie's embarrassed face ran south. He couldn't help but look at Elliot's open mouth and think dirty things. His heart picked up pace again, but faster than a flutter, more like a hum.

Elliot kept going, stroking his forefinger down from the base of his neck. His fingers got caught on his shirt, his partly undone shirt. He teased a glimpse of skin, smooth and taunt.

The blood running south accumulated in Donnie's cock. His pants were tight and constricting, and he shoved the bulge with his hand, trying to be subtle, but by Elliot's confident smile, he clearly knew he was having an effect on Donnie's cock.

Elliot's chest was rising and falling fast. He wasn't an exhausted mess like Donnie, but still panted. His heart must've been going fast too; his body must've been all sweaty beneath his shirt. Donnie didn't want to think about it, but he did.

Elliot looked infuriatingly gorgeous, and Donnie despised him for it.

"Want me to carry on?"

Donnie licked his lips. "I want you to die."

"It's only you and me up here."

Elliot undid another button. Despite his snarl, Donnie's eyes still feasted on the extra flesh. He remembered the smell of Elliot, a vanilla scent with a hint of spice.

"And another?"

Elliot's fingers picked at the next button, undoing it smoothly. He yanked his shirt to the side, exposing his pec and a pink and pointy nipple. Elliot rubbed his thumb over the nub, moaning softly.

Donnie swallowed and looked away.

"Wanna kill me, huh?"

"Yes," Donnie hissed.

"You're gonna have to try harder."

Elliot laughed, and Donnie risked looking at him. He'd stopped stroking his nipple and redid his buttons.

"You aching for me, baby?"

The teasing was over. Donnie surfaced from his desire, and all that filled his mind was the need to kill, the need to establish order and teach Elliot life's hardest lesson: how it felt to die.

Donnie drew his knees up to his chest, the movement acting as a distraction, and it seemed to work when Elliot didn't say anything.

"Don't you have somewhere to be?"

"I was having a lovely time shopping, but some asshole chased me, and I had to drop all my bags…"

Donnie sneaked his hand into his jacket pocket, out of view of Elliot. He grabbed the small switchblade and slowly withdrew it.

"Well, this was fun," Elliot said.

Donnie opened the knife. "Can't say I've enjoyed it."

"That's a shame."

"But I'm gonna enjoy this…"

He threw the knife at Elliot.

Donnie's sense of pride and cunning quickly went south, and he watched with a sense of horror as his attempt flopped like a limp dick. He barely threw the knife six feet, and they both watched as gravity claimed it.

The knife clanged when it met the ground, and slid noisily along the roof.

Elliot quirked his eyebrow. "That was…spectacular."

Donnie groaned and shuffled around until his back was to Elliot. "Get out of here, go on, get lost."

"Was that meant for me?"

"No."

Elliot kicked the knife. "It was, wasn't it?"

"Go away."

"Out of interest, have you ever killed anyone like that?"

"I have actually."

"I bet that was impressive."

Donnie shrugged. "I was pretty proud of it at the time."

"Now look how far you've fallen. What happened?"

Donnie didn't answer.

"Come on, tell me. What happened to the great Donnie King?"

"I messed up…"

"How?"

Donnie looked over his shoulder. "Like I'd tell you. And what about you? Why does Marco Russo want you dead so bad?"

Elliot flared his nostrils. "He can't want me dead that badly. He hired you…"

"You're a little shit."

"Yep. I'll leave you to it. Go home and have fun thinking of my dirty mouth, all sticky and wet."

"With blood," Donnie said, doing his best to drag his mind from the gutter.

"No, not with blood. With your come. Duh…your hot come dripping down my chin."

Donnie fidgeted, shaking his head. Blood rushed back and forth so fast in his body he was getting dizzy. In the end he was embarrassed and horny, and he goddamn hated the combo.

"There's only one more thing to say…"

"What?"

Donnie looked at Elliot, who winked.

"Bye, baby…"

He turned, ran to the edge of the roof, and jumped. He landed the other side, blew Donnie a kiss, then walked away.

Donnie fell back and ended up lying starfish on the roof. His pride and self-esteem was in tatters, but as he lay there, panting up at the sky, anger rekindled in his heart.

Elliot Austin had to die.

CHAPTER SEVEN

Donnie was dying. No doubt about it. His limbs were weak, he could barely lift his head, and he was crawling across the floor toward Ranger. He got to Ranger's feet and rested his burning hot head on his shoe, uttering pleas on his exhales.

Ranger laughed and nudged him with his foot.

"You okay down there, buddy?"

Donnie shook his head as much as he could. No, he was not okay. He was dying, and Ranger wasn't helping him.

Donnie wanted Ranger to help put him out of his misery, shoot him, but he didn't. He loomed over, chuckling.

"There's people looking over."

"I don't give a shit."

"A few are laughing."

"I'd prefer not to know."

"Christ."

Donnie face-planted the floor at Yates's voice.

"He was only on the machine for fifteen minutes," Ranger said.

"Hey," Yates said, kicking Donnie in the side.

Unlike Ranger, he wasn't gentle about it, and Donnie groaned. He rolled over onto his back and tried to stare up at them, but the room spun, and he could taste bile in the back of his throat. Exercise wasn't supposed to be that hard.

"You didn't kill him."

"He's superhuman, I swear."

He expected Yates to grimace, and boot him in the head, but instead a slow smile spread his lips.

"Elliot the Eagle."

"What?"

"Perhaps I should've mentioned, I did a bit of digging and found he's a parkour enthusiast."

"He—he's a free runner?"

"Oh yeah, loads of videos of him online. Gets members of the public to film him. They upload them under the tag 'Elliot the Eagle,' or at least he used to."

"And you didn't think to mention it?"

Yates shrugged. "I told you to get close to him and stab him, no mention of chasing him around the shopping mall."

"But…but…"

"So you still gonna kill Donnie for fucking up?"

Donnie tried to narrow his eyes at Ranger, but soon gave up when his head pounded. "Thanks a lot, buddy…but you know what, a bullet in the head right now would be a mercy."

Yates sighed. "Believe it or not, I can be a lenient man, and maybe I should've told you Elliot used to be rather athletic."

"He still is."

"So Donnie's got another chance?"

"Yes."

"I don't know whether to curse you or thank you."

Yates looked around the gym, then back down at Donnie hyperventilating on the floor. He knew he looked pathetic. A slight bit of exercise on the running machine and the thought of being shot was a nice one.

"This is your plan?" Yates said.

"Huh?"

"The gym."

"Yeah. I wanna get back to how I was, before…"

"You are rather unfit and pathetic at the moment."

"Thanks for that. I'm well aware of my slip in standards."

Yates nodded. "I'll help you."

"No, thanks."

"It wasn't an offer, but an order. I'll help you get back into shape, sort you out a fitness plan."

Ranger folded his arms. "And I'll get you shooting and stabbing efficiently."

"And together we'll get you ready for your next encounter with Elliot Austin."

Donnie rolled onto his side. "I'm gonna be sick…"

Ranger snorted, bumping his elbow into Yates. "God help us."

****

Red and yellow flashed behind Donnie's eyes. He gasped himself awake, then lay still staring at the ceiling. An echo of sound hit him, the smash of glass, the roar of fire, and the crunch of metal. His gut twisted, his stomach sloshed, and he remembered dropping to the ground, mouth hanging slack over what had just happened.

What he'd just done.

A car horn from outside helped him fully back to consciousness. He climbed out of bed and staggered into the bathroom.

The blast of hot water helped with the disgusted feeling which itched his skin, and the hissing sound stopped him hearing glass and fire on repeat.

He dried, got dressed, then wandered into the living room. His gaze found the whiskey bottle across the room. It was his normal go-to after he'd had a shit dream, and his tongue tingled with anticipation. He twitched his fingers at his sides, wanting to go over and have a glass but knowing he shouldn't.

In the end he settled for orange juice and toast before going for a run.

The morning air was welcome on his skin, and the slight wind cooled the sweat on his brow.

Four weeks since he'd last seen Elliot, and Yates was working him on the gym equipment like a dog. The first few days ended with him vomiting into a trash can while Yates yelled how pathetic he was.

He'd stopped throwing up, but the ache in his muscles didn't leave. On the hardest days, he crawled up the steps to his apartment on all fours. He looked more drunk than when he downed a whiskey bottle a day.

Ranger had him at the firing range every other day, different weapons, different distances before starting on moving targets. It was slow progress, not helped by the fact Donnie thought he was great at everything all until he tried to show his greatness, then realized he was shit. He was shit at everything.

Donnie had to get quicker, anticipate movement, and fire at the path ahead of his target. Donnie doubted he'd ever be gifted a shot like the one in the pancake house again. Elliot would keep moving.

Elliot Austin, or Elliot the Eagle as he was known online. He'd not uploaded a new video for a few years, but Donnie subscribed to his channel and watched all the videos of the blond who had humiliated the hell out of him.

The videos were all filmed from behind Elliot, following him as he flipped and twirled and jumped the seemingly impossible. His movements were fluid, like water with no gravity, twisting, turning, fascinating to watch.

Most of the videos he had his shirt off, and Donnie became transfixed by the look of his back, the tensing of his muscles, the stretch and twist of his skin. The way his sides looked when he took a deep breath in. He had a narrow waist and hips like handles, and when his flesh glimmered with sweat, it suited him.

Watching the videos was fast becoming an obsession, and he always turned them off when he became fixated on Elliot's ass and his cock started to stir. He would not jerk off to Elliot no matter how badly his cock desired it.

Donnie slowed his run when his phone vibrate against his thigh.

He sighed when he saw it was Yates.

"I'm running 3k right now."

"He's been spotted."

"Where?"

"Along the main street in Redding."

"He really is moving about the city…"

"Never stays in one place for long. He used his debit card in the convenience store at the end of Green Street."

"He was using cash before."

"Must've ran out."

Donnie narrowed his eyes. "How did you find him?"

"I have contacts all around, you know that. And one of them clocked him at the shopping mall weeks ago, but this time it was his bank activity. I've been monitoring it; knew he'd slip up at some point."

"Green Street?"

"Yep, get over there."

Yates hung up.

****

Donnie pushed the convenience store door open and did a quick scan of the area. Elliot wasn't in there, and Donnie didn't expect him to be. He spotted a camera in the corner of the shop and took a long hard look at it.

He walked up to the counter and presented the photograph of Elliot. The one that absolutely was not abused by Donnie's clutching fingers when he tried to think unsexy thoughts to not jerk off.

"He came in earlier."

The man nodded. "First time he's come in."

"He say anything, any hint to where he was staying?"

"No."

"What did he buy?"

"A pen."

Donnie frowned. "A pen, that's all?"

"Then he asked to pin something on the bulletin board."

Donnie spun around to find the board. In the center of the board were the words Bye, Baby written on a red splattered page. Donnie gawped at the bullet hole through the a on baby. The same page he'd shot at the pancake house.

"Little shit," he whispered.

Below the words was a number, and Donnie quickly typed it into his phone. He thought about calling it there and then but changed his mind.

He spoke over his shoulder to the man serving. "Thanks."

"Is he in trouble?"

Donnie snorted. "The worst kind."

He left the shop and jumped back into his car. He thought about calling the number while parked up on the curb but shook his head.

He wanted to get home first.

****

Donnie ran up the stairs to his apartment, no longer needing the railings to half heave himself up. He unlocked the door, slammed it shut behind him, then stared at the number on his phone.

Why would Elliot give him his number?

Donnie sighed heavily and sat down on the sofa. Despite the warning in his head telling him he shouldn't call and fall into Elliot's trap, he still pressed down on the number.

The call connected, but no voice came through from the other side.

Donnie looked at the seconds counting by on the screen before growling, "I'm gonna kill you."

"Oh, baby, thank god it's you."

"Don't call me baby."

"I've had a few phone calls from some major weirdos. It's a relief to finally hear your voice."

"Where are you?"

"In bed. Ready and waiting."

"What do you mean ready and waiting?"

"For your call of course. I know you're trying to find me. Thought I'd throw you a bone, and then you could sort mine out."

"What the hell are you talking about?"

"Tell me what you're gonna do to me."

Donnie scrunched up his face. "I'm gonna kill you."

"Yeah, but how?"

"I'm gonna put my gun to your head—"

Elliot grunted. "No, in my mouth, slip your gun into my mouth."

"Fine, in your mouth."

"Let me suck it, please."

"What?"

"I'd slip my tongue along the bottom of the barrel, quick little flicks. Would you like that?"

Donnie gawped. "Are you getting off right now?"

"You're saying you're gonna put your massive weapon in my mouth and let me suck it. Duh."

"No. I didn't say that—"

Elliot groaned. "Oh please let me suck it, only the tip, a little bit. I'll make it feel good, so good."

"Shut up."

"Shut me up. Put your cock into my mouth and stop me from speaking."

Donnie moved into the bedroom; he didn't know why exactly, but having Elliot talk to him like that in the living room seemed inappropriate. The blinds were all open, it was the middle of the day, birds were literally sitting on his windowsill. It was far more comfortable to lie on his bed and tell Elliot to shut up while he throttled his cock to stop it from growing.

"Do you like it nice and wet? All slobbery."

Donnie didn't answer. His cock was getting bigger in his pants whether he liked it or not.

"I'm not gonna jerk off to you."

"Yeah, you are."

"No."

"I'm soaking wet right now," Elliot whined. "Half a bottle of lube, poured all over my cock, balls, and hole. I've been edging myself for hours waiting for your call."

Donnie shivered at the imagery overload. He heard the breathlessness in Elliot's voice and the broken whimpers of pleasure.

"What are you wearing?"

Donnie shook his head. "I'm not doing this."

His hand was in his pants, rubbing the girth of his cock, but Elliot didn't know that, and Donnie wasn't going to give him the satisfaction of knowing.

"I'm wearing nothing, and I'm stroking myself real slow. I'm so fucking hard, baby. Every time the phone rang, I got harder, but now I know it's actually you, I can do something about it."

"You can stop playing with yourself and tell me where you are?"

"I can't stop. Touching myself and listening to your voice feels so good."

Donnie removed his hand from his pants. They were too tight; he needed them gone. He undid his buttons, shoved down his boxers, and released his eager hard-on. It jutted out, all big and proud of itself. Donnie narrowed his eyes at his traitorous body part. He wasn't supposed to get aroused by Elliot; his throbbing cock wasn't supposed to demand to be touched while he thought about him.

"Are you excited too?"

"No," Donnie growled. "You're not my type."

"I was your type the previous times we met."

He didn't touch his cock, but he stared at it bobbing, all desperate and eager and goddamn tragic. It dribbled onto his stomach, smearing in the hair leading from his crotch to his belly button. The sight and sensation filled his face with heat—the embarrassed, horny heat he'd come to associate with Elliot.

"I told you, I want you to die."

Elliot laughed, but it sounded strained, breathless. "That doesn't mean we can't indulge in a little stress relief."

Arousal throbbed in Donnie's cock. He glared at it, far too hot, and far too heavy. "I'm not stressed."

"Well, I am, so how's about I talk you through how I'm gonna unstress."

"No, thanks."

"You don't wanna hear me, then hang up."

Donnie puffed a furious breath through his nose. He couldn't hang up, not while Elliot was breathing funny and making cute little sounds of pleasure.

"Can you hear what I'm doing?" Elliot asked.

He couldn't hear the sound of Elliot's hand on his dick, but the sound of him breathing drove Donnie crazy.

Donnie's breathing got faster, and his heart drummed harder, punching in all his pulse points again. Another shiver went through his body, making his hairs stand on end.

"Answer or I'll hang up."

"Yes I can hear you."

Elliot chuckled. "It turning you on?"

"No, it's making me angry."

"Because you can't see or touch?"

"No, because you're still breathing."

Donnie gave his cock one quick tug. That was his cock's allowance, one tug, but precome dripped from the slit, then ran down the side in a thick teardrop. He ached, and he gripped onto the base to keep his cock slapping to his belly in frustration.

Elliot moaned. "I'm so fucking wet right now it's making me blush."

Donnie's cheeks were on fire. He didn't say anything but closed his eyes and fidgeted against the bed. He was only holding his cock. That's all it was—he wasn't stroking, wasn't getting any sense of pleasure from Elliot's teasing.

He was just keeping it still, holding it steady.

"I'm stroking myself, but I'm so slippery my cock keeps popping free. Can you hear it?"

Donnie concentrated and focused on the slick sounds coming through the phone. Elliot beating himself fast, then stopping, before beating fast again.

"Wait," he gasped.

Donnie licked his lips. "What?"

"I need both hands. I'm gonna put you on speaker."

Both hands on his cock, Donnie's brain flooded with desire. His cock tingled in his grip, and he gave in, giving it another quick tug, only halfway up, and not the head where he was most sensitive.

He was only adjusting his grip, that's all it was.

"Tell me how you want me to finish?" Elliot said.

Donnie squeezed his cock again and shook his head as if in pain. He didn't want to fall into Elliot's trap, but he was already halfway down, seduced by the sounds of him over the phone.

"You'll be finished when there's a gun to your head."

"No," Elliot panted. "I want it in my mouth. I want to suck on it so bad until it explodes, until it's all I can taste, all I'll ever taste. I want your gun's release smeared on my lips, in my hair. I want you to get me filthy."

"Fuck," Donnie said, pressing his head back into the pillow. He was stroking himself without even realizing it and stared accusingly at his cock and hand that seemed to have a mind of their own. They were siding with Elliot, the fucking enemy.

"I've got two hands. One's working my cock. Where do you want the other one?"

Donnie bit his lip until he tasted blood. He didn't want to answer. He was already jerking off, didn't want to give any more of his soul to Elliot by submitting to his teasing. He stroked the base of his cock, not his very filled, sensitive head.

"I could play with my nipples, or finger myself open, or cup my balls."

Donnie winced in pure agony—the agony of knowing failure was inevitable. He'd lost against Elliot yet again. He could feel the blood in his body filling his cock. He could feel the heaviness in his stomach, the need to give in to desire. The need to take control of Elliot.

"Speak or I hang up."

Donnie released his lip. "Touch your hole, press against the tightness."

Elliot's hum tapered off into a whimper. "I'm imagining it's you, baby. Tell me what you'd do."

"In and out—only the tip of one finger, but in and out, getting deeper each time."

"Fuck...feels good."

"Add another finger. Slide them in nice and slowly, feel every millimeter of my fingers going in."

Elliot whimpered. "Oh my god, Donnie. They're so big."

"That's why I'm going slow, letting you get used to them, letting you learn to love them."

"I fucking do."

Donnie hummed. "Push them deeper and keep them there."

Elliot groaned. "Then what?"

"Pump that beautiful cock of yours."

"Yeah?"

"Yeah. Fill yourself with fingers and pump your cock."

"Fuck! I'm doing it, baby."

"Come for me, Elliot."

Donnie's eyes fluttered shut when he heard Elliot's fast-beating hand. The wetness, the moans, the groans, before all went quiet. Donnie waited for it, the longest ten seconds of his life, then Elliot gasped, so sharp, it cut into Donnie's ears. He smiled, listening as Elliot took a few deep breaths, slowing himself down.

"That feel good?"

"Yeah," Elliot whispered. "Thank you."

Those two little words flipped Donnie's stomach, filling it with a lightness, a tingle like butterflies. He didn't know how to describe it, but

Elliot's soft voice thanking him was one of the hottest things he'd ever heard.

"I'm catching my breath, hold on," Elliot laughed. "That really took it out of me."

"Fuck," Donnie murmured, running his thumb up the sensitive seam of his cock. He'd resisted long enough but couldn't anymore. He started rubbing his pulsing cockhead, and it dribbled after each swipe. The thread of skin, so small and innocent-looking, held the electric nerves Donnie loved to play with. Hell, he loved others to play with it too, and right now it was Elliot's hand he imagined on him.

"Your turn," Elliot purred. "You almost there?"

Donnie pushed his hips off the bed, thrusting into his hand. He could feel the sheet of the mattress sticking to his lower back.

"Yeah," he admitted.

"I'll help you get there. I'll tell you what I'd do to you if I was there right now."

Donnie moaned, dignity gone. His greatest need was to come, to hell with everything else. His body demanded it.

"Tell me."

"I'd press my lips together as tightly as I could and drop down on your cock, force it to part my tight seal."

"Fuck, that's hot."

"I wouldn't loosen them though. I'd keep them tensed, clamping down on your cockhead as it pops inside."

"I love ass clamping down on me."

Donnie's eyes fluttered shut. He pictured Elliot's lips, imagined them all tight, him trying to deny him entry, but his cock penetrating them anyway.

"I'd keep my lips tight, tight like my little pink hole."

Donnie groaned, hating himself for it, but unable to stop his arousal being vocalized. He squeezed the top of his cock, rubbing the head between his thumb and forefinger, imagining he was sinking into Elliot's tight entrance. He imagined the resistance, the pressure before Elliot's body adjusted to his girth. He imagined his pink lips keeping tight around him, while his wicked wet tongue prodded his slit.

"That's it," Elliot cooed. "Imagine my mouth on your cock, my warm wet mouth. Imagine my ass on your cock, swallowing it up. Imagine how fucking good I'd feel."

Donnie imagined them separately, then all at once. Elliot's ass, his mouth, his ass, his mouth, his ass.

Both tight, and hot, and wet.

"Do I feel good, Donnie?"

"So fucking good."

Donnie flung his head back, lifted his hips off the bed, and crushed his cockhead as he succumbed to the fire. His whole body spasmed with the force of the orgasm. Three powerful squirts left him with a messy torso, and the rest ran over his fingers.

Pleasure washed over him in waves, lessening in intensity as he came back to earth.

"That was hot," Elliot said.

Donnie sunk back down, dropping his cock. "I can't wait to kill you."

"You gotta catch me first," Elliot smirked, then whispered. "Bye, baby."

The line went dead.

CHAPTER EIGHT

Yates squeezed the bridge of his nose. "There was no sign of him?"

Donnie couldn't look Yates in the eye, and instead spoke to the closest vase of flowers. They were blush-pink roses according to the label.

"No. I asked about him in the shop. That was the first time he's gone in."

"What did he buy?"

Donnie scratched the back of his head. "Huh?"

"You heard what I said."

"A pen."

Yates frowned at the floor. "A pen."

"Yep."

"But why?"

Donnie's cheeks started to prickle, and a heat swept over him. He didn't answer Yates's question, hoping it was rhetorical, and carried on staring at the roses. A subtle shade of pink, a similar same shade as Elliot's pert lips. Donnie's cheeks caught fire.

"He risked exposing himself for a pen?"

Donnie swallowed. "Looks that way."

Yates shook his head. "No."

"No?"

"He keeps a low profile, hasn't used his bank card at all until yesterday to buy a goddamn pen. It's not adding up."

"It does seem a little strange."

Yates balled his hand into a fist. "He wanted to be found. It's a taunt. He's confident he can get away. Bastard."

The bell to the shop rang, and Donnie had never been more relieved to see Ranger. He swaggered in, sliding his glasses up into his hair.

"My bitches are looking tense."

Yates wagged a finger at him. "Don't start."

"I take it the kid's still alive?"

"There was no sign of him when I got there."

Instead there was a notice on the board, telling Donnie to call him. Donnie, who indulged in an unusual bit of stress relief. It was the first time he'd had phone sex with a man he was trying to kill.

Ranger shrugged. "Shame."

"He's taunting us though," Yates said.

"How?"

"He bought a pen."

Ranger's lips parted. "No way. Was it your favorite pen?"

"Ranger…" Yates growled.

"Did you want the pen? Did he buy the last one? Did you cry sad tears?"

"Think very carefully about annoying me right now."

"Oh, relax," Ranger said, jumping up to sit on one of the display tables. "Explain why him buying a pen is so offensive?"

"He's not an easy man to find, then uses his card at a corner shop to buy a pen. Puts a spotlight on himself for no reason."

"He could've just needed a pen. Anyway, I've got more pressing matters."

"Which are?" Donnie asked.

"I need you to look at my dating profile and tell me what you think."

Yates huffed. "Dating?"

"Ranger's decided he wants a boyfriend."

"You hurt your head more than I thought."

Ranger slipped his phone from his pocket and handed it to Donnie. "What do you think of my profile pic?"

"If it's not a crotch shot, then what's the point," Yates muttered.

Ranger wore his leather jacket in the photo, unzipped with no T-shirt underneath. His head was to the side, showing the snake tattoo on his head. His lips were parted, and he didn't look directly at the camera.

"You look kinda like a stripper."

Ranger bunched his lips together, seemingly deciding whether to feel offended or not.

He smiled. "A high-end stripper."

"Yeah, why not," Donnie said, handing the phone back.

"I'm happy with that. I've already got a few messages."

"What did they say?"

"They didn't say anything. They were dick pics."

"Nice dicks?" Yates asked.

Ranger shrugged. "I wouldn't say no."

A grumble left Yates. "Perhaps dating sites aren't a bad idea."

Donnie rolled his eyes. "The point is to 'date' not exchange dick pics."

"Get with the twenty-first century. That's modern-day dating. When was the last time you got some action?"

Donnie looked away quickly. He pictured Elliot's lips, remembered the feel of them when they kissed, and then his mind took him on a different tangent. He imagined Elliot's lips tense, him keeping them tight as he pressed his dick forward. Mouth, ass, mouth, ass. Donnie imagined them all together.

"The last action you got was kissing my shoe," Yates said.

Ranger burst out laughing. "I can't believe you crawled across the floor and kissed Yates's shoes."

"I'm concentrating on getting myself back into shape so I never have to grovel like that again."

Ranger looked him up and down. "It's working."

"Thanks—"

"I mean, it's slow progress, really slow, but it is progress. That's the point."

Donnie glared at Ranger, then shook his head. "Thanks for that."

"You're most welcome."

"You're fucking kidding me," Yates said sharply.

Donnie turned to him. "What?"

"You got your gun on you?"

"No—"

"Ranger?"

"Nope."

"You're both useless. Let's play this cool."

"Play what?" Donnie asked.

The bell to the shop rang. Three smartly dressed men stepped inside. The one in the middle cleared his throat. Tall, bald, with intensely staring eyes. His gaze roamed the shop, and he flashed a look at Donnie, a slightly longer one at Ranger before fixing his narrowed eyes to Yates.

He cracked his neck, still glaring Yates down. "Marco called me."

"Don't you mean us? There's three of you," Ranger said.

"Lower the blinds."

Both men accompanying him lowered a blind either side, then stood back at attention.

"I'm Christian."

"Christian Black. I know who you are," Yates growled.

"Then you know what this means."

Ranger held up his hands. "Well, I don't."

"Shut your pet up, or I'll shut him up for you."

Ranger opened his mouth to reply, but Yates snapped his fingers and he fell silent.

Christian tilted his head toward the man on the left. "This is Greg."

Long hair, a goatee, hands shoved in his jacket. He had a grin slapped to his face and kept snorting softly under his breath.

"And Nigel."

The other man was short and quiet, watching Yates but with less intensity.

"Nice to meet you, fellas," Ranger said, holding his hand out to Nigel.

Nigel looked at Ranger's outstretched hand, frowned, then reattached his gaze to Yates.

"Well, that's rude."

Christian tilted his head the other way, toward Ranger, but kept his sights on Yates. "I know you took a bullet to the head a few years back, but I won't hesitate to do it again."

"Maybe I'll get my memories back."

"Or maybe I'll splatter the rest of your brains across the floor."

Ranger sighed. "Yeah, that's a possibility too."

"Donnie King." Christian snorted.

His name got a reaction from both Greg and Nigel. Greg snorted louder, and Nigel's serious expression broke into a smile before going serious again. Once his name had been envied, once it had been inspiring, but now in their world it was a joke—he was a joke.

"I thought you were dead."

"Not yet."

"I've always thought it's better to die when you're at the top of your game than fall and become a ghost of yourself. You've proved my thought correct."

Ranger pushed out his chest. "Donnie's making a comeback."

"It's impossible to climb yourself out of pig-shit slurry."

"You'd know."

Christian grimaced, showing his teeth. "Yeah, I do. I've drowned a few in it. Nigel. Greg."

Both Greg and Nigel pulled their guns out. Greg pointed his at Donnie, and Nigel pointed his at Ranger. They both stood awkwardly, horribly exposed and helpless in the situation. Donnie's heart rate started to gather pace. He looked at the gun, then Greg.

Greg was still snorting soft laughs. His eyebrows twitched, and his hand tremored slightly, not with nervousness, but anticipation. It was Donnie's luck to get the trigger-happy one.

"Are you fond of your friends?" Christian asked Yates.

"Not particularly."

"So it doesn't matter if I shoot them?"

"Couldn't care less about them, but my flowers. I wouldn't want them sprayed with blood and brains. Not to mention it's the middle of the day, you don't have silencers fitted, and even if you did, the shots would still be heard. There's a camera outside too, recording anyone who walks inside. So the three of you would be kinda screwed."

"I didn't see a camera."

"It's there."

Christian blinked for the first time since he walked inside the shop. Yates's shoulders dropped, and he loosened his crossed arms.

"Why are you here?" he asked.

"Marco's asked me to carry out the hit too. So you've got competition for that 200K."

Donnie frowned fiercely, looking at Yates. Yates didn't spare him a glance, and Christian and him went for round two of their psychopath staring contest.

"You're no competition."

"So you've killed him, then?"

Yates flared his nostrils.

"Thought not."

Christian turned the door on the sign to Closed, then locked the door. He pulled a rose out of the closest bunch, shoved his nose inside, and took a deep inhale.

Yates didn't comment, but Ranger snorted softly.

"Something funny?"

"No, it's the flower— like an asshole—never mind."

"There's a gun pointed at your head right now."

"I know."

"Don't test me."

Ranger looked as if he was about to speak, but Donnie shook his head.

"Looks like you lot have lost your touch, Yates. Can't even kill a kid. I mean, I'd understand if it was Donnie struggling."

"I'm biding my time," Yates said,

"Elliot's gallivanting around the city, burning through all Marco's money while you allow it. Marco's so angry he's frothing at the mouth. I told him not to worry, I'll end Elliot Austin, and end anyone that gets in my way."

"Are you really that stupid to threatening me? In my own shop."

"It's a flower shop, and you're outgunned." Christian started pulling petals off the rose. "I'm a good sport though. I've told you what's gonna happen, so you can back off."

"Back off?"

"Yes, leave this hit to the professionals."

"You, Greg, and Nigel?"

"And the others."

"Others? How many of you are there?"

"Five or so. Get in our way and you'll end up dead. This is a friendly warning: next time we see each other, it might be a quite different outcome. Do the sensible thing and back off."

"No chance."

"You'll end up dead."

"Then I'll make sure I take you with me."

Christian grinned, nodded, then walked backward toward the door. Greg and Nigel put their guns away, and all three of them left.

Ranger hopped back up on the table as if nothing had happened. "So under occupation, what do you think I should put?"

"Professional idiot." Donnie huffed before looking at Yates. "200K? The hit on Elliot is for 200K?"

"Yes."

"You said it was for 50K and you were taking sixty percent."

"He was my hit; I was doing you a favor. I'd be 200K richer now if it wasn't for your seductive begging. Not only that, but now there's a team of assholes after Elliot as competition."

"You lied about the money, didn't tell me about the parkour."

"I don't have to be honest with you, Donnie, you're not my mother. I've got to find Elliot and sort this out fast."

"He's mine—"

"No he's not."

"You gave him to me!"

"I'm taking him back."

Ranger whistled. "Calm down, bitches."

Yates glared at him. "Ranger, I swear to god—"

"There's no need to fight over the cute blond when you can both have him. The way I see it, they've got a team to kill Elliot, so you need a team, right?"

Yates nodded patronizingly slow. "Yes, that would be useful, a team of master assassins, but unfortunately all I see is a has-been and a…a…" He looked at Ranger. "And a been-had."

Ranger frowned. "I should be offended, but I'm not."

"The old Ranger would've thrown something across the room by now," Donnie said.

"Like a flower?"

"Like a fucking vase or a knife."

Ranger turned to Yates. "We're already working as a team to get Donnie back into shape."

"I only offered to see him suffer."

"Sadistic bastard," Donnie muttered.

"We need to get his hand to hand up to scratch too for him to be of any use."

Donnie snorted. "My hand to hand is fine."

Ranger looked at him, then launched a punch his way. He'd been expecting it, but still didn't move fast enough to avoid it. Ranger hit Donnie in the chest, and he dropped to his knees gasping for breath.

"I'd be happy to help Donnie with hand to hand," Yates said, grinning.

"So it's agreed, then," Ranger said. "The three of us can find, catch, and kill Elliot before Christian and his minions. We'll split the money between the three of us, and everyone's happy…or as happy as you can possibly be, Yates."

"Please say I'm not gonna regret this."

"No more than giving Donnie your easy hit."

Yates groaned. "Fine, I'm in. Let's kill this kid."

"Donnie?"

He swallowed the lump in his throat. "Let's find him."

CHAPTER NINE

Donnie stood in front of his bathroom mirror. For the first time in months, he actually looked at himself. He could see the faint outline of muscle on his abdomen—not what he used to have, but definitely an improvement. His biceps and triceps were bigger from all the weight lifting at the gym.

He no longer got out of breath climbing the steps to his apartment, and even after a long run his sides didn't burn from exertion.

He looked in the mirror and started to like what he saw. Not only that, but he started to feel better on the inside, less cloggy, looser, dare he say it, but in a sense, happier.

He trimmed his beard, swept wax into the long fringe of his hair, then rubbed moisturizer onto his face.

Donnie looked more and more like the old Donnie King.

There were still bags under his eyes, but he couldn't control his dreams. The explosion always woke him up in a hot sweat. That was something that didn't plague the old Donnie but would always plague the new one.

He'd always have haunted eyes.

Donnie grabbed his shirt hanging on the back of the door. He buttoned it over his improving physique before slapping aftershave onto his neck.

It had been four weeks since he'd called Elliot, four weeks since Christian had made his interest in Elliot known.

Donnie had Elliot's number, but when he called it, no one answered. It went straight to voicemail. He didn't know what to say, caught in two minds of wanting a repeat, and wanting Elliot dead.

Donnie's phone started buzzing by the sink, pulling him from his thoughts.

"Yates?"

"I've found him."

"Where?"

"Oak Ridge, north side of the river. I've got him on CCTV enjoying the sunshine, sitting on a bench facing the river."

"You're watching all the CCTV now?"

"I have an extensive list of contacts searching for him. He's good at keeping a low profile when he wants to which is why this seems like a taunt yet again. CCTV right by him, he knows he'll be spotted. Knows someone will come for him."

"He likes the chase."

"He won't like it when you catch him and put a bullet through his head."

****

The place was packed, parking was a nightmare, but finally Donnie was strolling the street, heading toward the bench Elliot had been sitting on.

He couldn't believe his luck when Elliot was still there, facing the river, unaware of Donnie creeping up behind him. Elliot had his phone out and looked as if he was taking photos of the scenery.

"Nice of you to join me," he said, rising from the bench.

Donnie rocked back on his heels. "How'd did you—"

"Internal camera."

"Ah."

"I've been waiting for two hours."

"You've gotta find something better to do with your time."

Elliot snorted. "Isn't that the truth. I like the outfit."

Donnie had smartened his look up, no longer rushing after Elliot in a stained T-shirt and worn jacket. He was back to his stylish suits, and wearing them again felt good, felt right.

"I thought you might have given up on me."

Donnie frowned. "Why do you say that?"

"I had someone else following me the last few days. Gave him the slip a few times."

"I'm not the only person after you."

Elliot raised his eyebrows. "How interesting."

"I'm gonna be the one to kill you though."

"Let's get to it, then," Elliot said, smiling.

"Yes, let's."

Elliot took off, and Donnie gave chase. It was a flat out run along the river, and Donnie kept pace, matched Elliot's speed until he could almost reach him. Elliot stopped and ducked, before running the other way.

Donnie followed. Elliot ducked and retraced their steps.

Every time Donnie started to close in, Elliot changed direction sharply, leaving Donnie clutching air. It was like a frustrating cartoon sketch; he could never catch the irritating blond mouse no matter how hard he tried, or how close he got. They ran back and forth along the river, until Donnie cursed at the sky. He was supposed to be a professional hit man, and there he was, practically playing a game of tag by the river.

When he turned around, Elliot had gone.

"What the hell."

He looked around; he couldn't see Elliot across the road. There was no mop of blond hair rushing away.

Donnie froze at the roar of a boat engine. Donnie peered over the edge to see Elliot on a small speedboat. He had his hand on the driver's shoulder and was grinning up at Donnie. The cocky shit had set a getaway up to leave him humiliated…again.

Elliot tapped his wristwatch. "This was fun, but I gotta go. We should do it again sometime."

Donnie gritted his teeth. "Little shit."

"Bye, baby!"

The boat took off across the river, leaving Donnie standing on the bank with his head in his hands.

"Donnie!"

He spun around to see Ranger on his bike.

"Yates called me."

"You beauty," Donnie gasped, rushing forward.

"Me or the bike?"

"I could kiss you both right now."

"Please don't."

Donnie jumped onto the back, then clung on for life. He tried to keep his eyes on the river, pinpointing the boat in the distance. Elliot wouldn't be expecting him to turn up on the other side; he had no idea Donnie had caught a ride.

Donnie could see Elliot strolling across the road, heading toward the shops. He was looking at his phone, guard completely down.

He tapped Ranger on the shoulder, and he pulled up on the side.

Donnie jumped off the back of the bike. "Thanks!"

"Get him, tiger."

He took off down the street with the excited thump of his heart fueling his veins. His shoes slapped along the pavement. Elliot looked up, turned around, and Donnie went straight into him, slamming him to the ground.

Elliot grunted in pain, trying to struggle away, but Donnie pinned him by the wrists. He finally had hold of him, had finally caught him.

"Got you!"

Elliot looked up at him with wide, shocked eyes. Donnie's heart pounded fast, and he swore he could feel Elliot's pulse beating in his wrists. His gaze found Elliot's inviting pink lips, and he swallowed. He wasn't supposed to be looking at his mouth, wasn't supposed to be thinking about it, but there he was, staring, thinking about it, and he leaned down a fraction, unsure of what he was about to do.

"Is there a problem?"

Donnie blinked, then raised his head and looked at the two men approaching. Both with ripped physiques and sports bags on their backs. Donnie looked beyond them to the sign for the twenty-four-hour gym.

"Help!" Elliot shouted. "Please help me!"

Donnie looked down at him, blubbering, with tears clinging to his lashes. He was shaking, cowering, or trying his best to while pinned by his wrists.

"You little—"

"Please, I told him no, but he won't leave me alone."

The gym buddies dropped their bags to the ground at exactly the same time.

"I think you better get off him."

The commotion gathered a crowd of onlookers. There was no chance Donnie was going to be able to drag Elliot off somewhere without being seen.

Donnie relaxed his grip on Elliot's wrists. "Look—"

"No, you look. Let him go."

"He's my ex! He's been stalking me, swearing he'll kill me if I don't take him back."

A woman in the crowd got her phone out, and Donnie swore she mentioned the word police. Donnie stood up and held his hands up to appease the two men circling him. He stepped away from Elliot, which appeared to be what the two men were waiting for.

The first fist he managed to dodge, but the second caught him on the cheekbone. He staggered back, rubbing his face.

"Must we do this?" he asked.

"Yes, we must."

Donnie nodded. "Okay then."

He couldn't dodge and twist like Elliot could, but he was gifted with a mean right hook. No booze to cloud his judgment, and with adrenaline fueling his body, he went on the offensive.

His body ran on autopilot; a whole skill set of moves to pacify an opponent were at his disposal. Both Ranger and Yates had been helping his combat moves. Yates just used it as an excuse to beat the shit out of him.

Donnie launched at the first man, kicking his knee out, elbowing him in the ribs before finishing with his tidy right hook. A nice little sequence that took the muscular man down effortlessly.

The next man went down even easier—one blow to the stomach, then one to the side of his head. He collapsed groaning on the floor, and the crowd of people around them all took a few steps back.

Donnie spun around to face Elliot, but he wasn't on the floor anymore. He was on his feet, jumping up and down on the spot and beckoning for Donnie to follow him.

"Come get me."

****

There was something exhilarating about chasing Elliot down. Donnie had chased down others before, but the way Elliot moved, his twists and turns and jumps, they were majestic, hypnotic. Despite Donnie's aching legs and his burning lungs, he kept pursuing. He didn't allow Elliot to leave his sight.

More than once he found himself appreciating Elliot's flexing ass. He'd been thinking more and more about his ass the last few days.

Donnie didn't know how they ended up in a closed-down clinic. He didn't question it, just allowed Elliot to lead him. They were running down a litter-strewn corridor. Graffiti had been sprayed over graffiti, and every inch of the walls and ceiling had been covered, making it feel claustrophobic and trippy.

Elliot shot through the door at the end, then slammed it shut. Donnie got to it, tried to shove it open, but Elliot pushed against the other side. "Wait, wait, wait!"

Donnie took a step back. "Why?"

"You winded me earlier."

"Good."

"And I'm guessing you're kind of tired too?"

Donnie was full-on heaving. "What's your point?"

"We could have a little break, a rest stop."

"What do you suggest, we go get a smoothie together?"

"Don't be daft. I mean here. Let's sit for a minute."

Donnie heard what sounded like Elliot slipping down the door, then grunting when his ass met the floor.

"A minute," Donnie said.

"Two."

"Fine, a two-minute rest."

Donnie turned around and slid down the door. He was breathing heavily, but it was at least a relief to hear Elliot panting for breath on the other side. He touched his tender cheek, wincing.

"I wasn't expecting the motorbike," Elliot said.

"I wasn't expecting the boat."

Elliot laughed. "Should've seen your face."

"I imagine it looked the same as yours when I pinned you to the ground."

"A mixture of surprise, and holy shit that's hot."

Donnie rolled his eyes.

"You wanted to kiss me; I could tell."

"No, I wanted to stick my gun between your lips and blow your brains out."

"We both know you mean the gun in your pants, not the bang-bang kind."

"You're mistaken. I told you, you're not my type."

"I loved you on top of me like that, pinning me, making me helpless. It did things to me, made me feel all funny inside."

It did things to Donnie too, but he'd rather die than admit it.

"You loved it so much you screamed for help."

"You taking those two guys out was the hottest thing ever. I had to run away with my hard-on chafing against my pants. You're looking fine, baby."

"Whatever."

"I mean it. You're like a fucking phoenix rising from the ashes. I'm so proud of you."

Donnie knocked the back of his head to the door. "I can't wait to kill you."

"That's not very nice. I was giving you a compliment, the least you can do is give me one back. Come on, try and say something nice."

"Okay. I'm looking forward to seeing your cute face again."

Elliot laughed. "Aww, there ya go—"

"With a bullet hole through it."

"You evil, evil man."

"Was that not nice enough for you?" Donnie asked.

"We both know you don't spend your nights picturing that kind of hole…it's another hole you're interested in. Actually, there's two holes of mine you're interested in."

Donnie licked his lips.

"I've got a lot of missed calls from you, baby…"

"To find out where you were—"

"Or you wanted more sexy times but were too afraid to ask."

"No."

Elliot laughed. "Then why didn't you give up my phone number, huh?"

"What?"

"This guy you've got tracking me, sending my picture out in the city, watching my card purchases, and all the CCTV. He knows what he's doing—or knows the people that can do it for him, but you didn't give up my number. He could easily track me with it."

"I didn't know that."

"Yes you did. Maybe you're not ready for that bullet in my head yet."

"You've lost your mind. The first chance I get—"

"Maybe you're liking the chase as much as I am. Maybe I'm good for you."

"Good for me?"

"Do you remember what you looked like when we first met?"

Donnie grimaced. He tried not to think about it. He felt dirty when he did, like a sudden layer of filth had just infected him.

"Tatty hair, boozed up, a dead weight. Now look at you."

Donnie may've been breathing heavily, but he wasn't crawling along the floor like when he'd started going to the gym again. In fact, their run across the city had made him feel good.

"You've cut your hair; you're getting into shape. Not to mention the defeat I saw in your face. Now there's fire, purpose."

"I've got to admit the thought of killing you has been a huge incentive for me to get my shit together."

"Ha! Told you so. I'm good for you."

Donnie chuckled, shaking his head.

"And you're good for me."

Elliot said it so quietly Donnie almost missed it.

"How the hell am I good for you? I'm trying to kill you."

"It's messed up but…"

"But what?"

"It kind of makes me feel wanted."

Donnie turned his head and stared accusingly at the door. There was no humor in Elliot's voice, only sadness. Something sharp dug into Donnie's chest.

"That is messed up."

"I know, right, but it's like I'm important, like I matter. Someone hunting me down, trying to find me, trying to catch me—"

"I'm trying to kill you."

"I know, okay. I said it was messed up."

"How did you get involved with Marco Russo?"

"You wouldn't believe me if I told you."

"Try me?"

"Are we really gonna do a heart-to-heart?"

Donnie shrugged, knocking the back of his head to the door again. "Why not?"

Elliot was silent for a long time, then mumbled, "He's my dad."

"What?"

"I'm the son he wished he never had."

"I—I don't understand—"

"Well, he fucked my mom."

"That's not what I meant."

"My mom was a dancer back in the day when Marco was rising through the ranks. I'm a one-night-stand baby. When he found out my mom was expecting, he was furious, he tried to make her get rid of me. She ran away from the city, her home. He sent people after us, but we kept moving around, kept hiding from him. Eventually he stopped, but my mom never stopped moving, never trusted anyone, and I'm the same. Now she's gone, and I'm done hiding. I found him, watched him, learned about him, his businesses, his practices, his contacts. That's how I knew about you."

"What did you hear about me exactly?"

"You were the best in the business, and hot as anything. Some guy said you were the best he's ever had; you can go for hours apparently."

"What guy?"

"I think it was Vince, or Vinnie."

"Ah, good old Vinnie."

"Hey, I'm right here." Elliot banged on the door. "I don't want to hear you reminiscing over your past conquests. It makes me jealous, makes me want to do something reckless like open this door and climb on your lap."

"Why don't you?"

"You don't get me that easily, baby. I don't quite know how to tell you this, but 'good old Vinnie' is now dead Vinnie."

"What?"

"My dad killed him after he found out he'd been talking to me. He doesn't want anyone to know who I am, that I'm his. I disgust him, and to make him hate me that little bit more, I broke into his place and stole a shitload of his money."

Donnie snorted. "I heard."

"Jumped the fence, avoided the cameras, outran the dogs, and got into his office."

"You'd make a good assassin."

"Thanks. I tried to convince myself it was revenge, that he owes me, but that's a lie."

"Then why do it?"

"I wanted to mean something to him, and now I do. Now he does want me. He wants me so badly he sends people after me, and then they want me too to fill their pockets with cash."

"Marco wants you dead. He's always wanted you dead."

"Want is want in whatever capacity. I'm on his radar again, on his mind, tormenting his thoughts like he's done to me my whole life. He wants me dead, and you want to kill me for his cash. That's two men that want me, and even in this messed-up way, it's nice to be wanted. I want to feel wanted."

His last words sounded so small, so fragile, Donnie mouthed at air, thinking of something to say.

"What happened to your mom?"

"She died a few years back now. She taught me some good lessons: never trust anyone, never let anyone know your desires or secrets, keep to yourself, keep a low profile, keep moving to stay alive."

"So you stole from Marco, the mad mafia guy."

Elliot clacked his tongue to the roof of his mouth. "Not all of my mom's wisdom sunk in. I've spilled my guts; now it's time for you to do the same."

Donnie's stomach started to churn. The happy feeling of that morning faded; the looseness tightened until he was choked by his memories. He didn't want to sink under again.

His throat dried until he could barely swallow. He needed to go home—he needed a whiskey.

"Donnie?"

Elliot had shared something painful with him; it was only fair he did the same.

"Why did you lose your way?"

"I messed up."

"Your target got away?"

"No, I completed the hit."

"I don't understand."

Donnie closed his eyes. "I rigged a car, watched from the end of the road. He came out, but his nine-year-old daughter was with him. I'd been watching the house for days; every other day she'd waited for the school bus, but she got in her dad's car that morning."

"Shit."

"She was smiling when she got in the car—they both were. I couldn't do anything to stop it, but I made myself watch. I had to make sure I saw the gravity of what I'd done to her. My moral code isn't perfect—it's by no means clean—but not children. Never children. Her smiling face plagues my dreams. I see the explosion, hear the sound, can practically feel the heat."

"I wish I could tell you it wasn't your fault. It was, but—"

"There are no buts. I killed a child."

"You couldn't have known she was going to get in the car that day."

"I still did it though. I still killed her, blew her to pieces along with her father. I've been asked to kill children and families before, always refused. Found those assassins that did disgusting animals, and then I became one of them."

"You're not like them."

"Of course I am, and no one will convince me otherwise."

"So you drank yourself into a slumber."

"That's it in a nutshell, yeah."

"Why? You can't change what happened. You can't bring her back."

"I guess it's punishment."

Elliot didn't say anything, and the silence lingered. Donnie's eyes prickled with shame, threatening to spill over.

"That's heavy," Elliot said finally. "Almost as heavy as you when we first met."

The despair threating to pull Donnie under faded. The tension cut, and the dark cloud closing in on him stopped.

He laughed, wiping his eyes.

"You're a little shit."

"I had to heave you into that chair. Pulled a muscle in my back doing it."

"Then you climbed on my lap and kissed me."

Elliot hummed. "I enjoyed that kiss. Your little gasp of surprise when I caught you off guard, and that anger surging into your mouth. It was hot despite the grubby hair, and the alcohol breath, and the razor stubble—"

"Okay, okay, I get it."

"You looked rough, seriously rough, almost like a corpse."

"You have a habit of kissing corpses?"

"Of course not. Just the hot ones, recently deceased via frying pan skills."

"You hit me pretty damn hard."

"I seriously thought you were dead at one point."

"I think I was getting there before I met you."

"Then I kinda saved your life."

"I'm still gonna end yours though."

Elliot laughed. "I think our two minutes are up."

"I think so too."

Donnie got to his feet.

"Let's do this, baby."

Donnie flung open the door. "Don't call me baby."

"I spy stairs!"

Dread twisted in Donnie's stomach. He knew what Elliot was gonna do once he got to the top of them, and when he burst open a door to the roof, Donnie groaned.

"That's unfair."

He rushed after Elliot and watched the eagle in action.

He sprinted to the edge of the roof and leapt. He landed on the other side, rolled, then stood up. Elliot turned around with his hands on his hips and walked closer with a confident swagger.

Donnie approached the edge of the roof, shaking his head.

"Come on, I don't have all day…" Elliot said.

Donnie narrowed his eyes at Elliot's grinning face.

"Hand on heart. I will honestly not catch you."

Donnie looked at the alley below; he must've been three floors up. The drop wasn't deadly but was definitely a leg breaker. He breathed deep, then took a few strides back from the edge.

"Yes, baby! You can do it—or you can't. Only one way to find out."

"You're a parkour expert."

"Expert? I like that, thank you. Have you been watching my videos?"

"A few."

"And what did you think?"

Donnie shook his head. "Impressive."

"Some good views of my ass, huh? I ask strangers to film me on my phone, but sometimes they're massive perverts and do close-ups of my ass. Do you know the videos I'm talking about?"

Donnie was pretty damn sure he did. He was also drawn to Elliot's ass, wanted to spread it, kiss it, lick it, toy with it until he was satisfied.

He bit the inside of his cheek. "Shut up. I'm trying to concentrate."

"You make the jump and you can pick whatever hole you want."

Donnie tried to block Elliot out, but it was impossible when he started jumping up and down on the other roof.

"Come get me!"

Donnie breathed out sharply and started running. His thighs were burning, his sides screamed in protest, and he didn't breathe as he ran to the edge.

He was about to make the greatest leap in his comeback yet.

His shoulder smashed into concrete, his hip flared with pain, and a chin knocked into his, making his teeth click together. There was a growl, not his own, and then Ranger's face appeared in front of his, full-on raging. For the first time since Ranger had been shot in the head, Donnie saw his seething rage.

"Have you lost your damn mind!"

Donnie's head spun. Ranger pinned him and was yelling in his face. He had his fists scrunched in Donnie's shirt and shook him like a rag doll. Donnie grabbed onto his wrists, trying to ease him off, but it only infuriated Ranger further. He released Donnie's jacket and went for his throat instead.

"Kill you myself."

Donnie kneed Ranger in the side, tipping him off. He kept his grip on Donnie's throat though, strangling him.

"Let go," Donnie gasped, battling with Ranger's hands.

Ranger flared his nostrils, red veins popped in his eyes.

"Donnie!"

It was Elliot's voice, and he sounded panicked.

Donnie smacked the heel of his hand into Ranger's nose, once, twice, until blood gushed out, and Ranger blinked. He released Donnie's throat, and he crawled away, gasping and spluttering.

Ranger wiped his nose on the back of his arm, then stared at the bloody smear. He looked over to Donnie, and the rage was gone. He looked confused and rolled his fingers against his temples.

"We good now?" Donnie croaked.

Ranger nodded. "What were you thinking?"

"That I could make the jump."

"I'm the one with half a brain, not you."

"Where did you come from?"

"Fucking Mars as far as you're concerned, but I've saved your legs." Ranger looked up. "You let Elliot goad you into it. You let him coax you into jumping."

Donnie got shakily to his feet, still wary of Ranger.

"I would've made it." He turned to the other roof, but Elliot had gone. "I could've got him. I could've finished it."

"No, you would've fallen and snapped both your ankles. You know Yates has got no bedside manner whatsoever. He would've smothered you with your hospital pillow for being so stupid, and I would've let him."

Ranger stood up. He wiped his dirty hands over his knees, then hissed when he caught sight of his bloodied elbow. Donnie saw it too and winced.

"I'm sorry about your elbow, but not about the nose."

Ranger offered his hand to Donnie.

"I'm sorry about whatever that was."

"And what was it?"

Ranger shook his head. "I don't know, Donnie, but I couldn't stop. I couldn't hold it back."

"That was the old Ranger for sure. Raging Ranger."

"I'm glad he's gone."

They both approached the edge of the building.

"I lost Elliot again."

"I think it's not a case of you losing him, more him getting away. He's a special one, isn't he?"

"He sure is," Donnie whispered.

CHAPTER TEN

Donnie glared at Ranger while doing his cooldown exercises. His muscles were all humming with the familiar ache of a vigorous workout. It was a pleasant buzzing all through his body. The only thing killing the mood was Ranger.

Ranger had told Yates what had happened on the rooftop as soon as he'd come into the gym. Donnie thought Yates would punch him in the gut, or at the very least trip him up on the running machine, but he didn't say or do anything.

The silence was somehow worse. Yates was brooding, going about his routine with barely a sound. Even his grunts of exertion were muted compared to what they usually were. Ranger kept bringing it up, clearly wanting some kind of explosive reaction.

"He wouldn't have made it."

Donnie groaned. "Yes, I would have. Now stop going on about it."

"No you wouldn't."

"Yes I—"

"Enough!" Yates shouted.

Donnie readied himself for it, the fist, the kick, the whip of Yates's sweaty towel, something, but instead Yates turned away from them and walked over to the mats.

"You've been arguing about it all morning, and it's given me a headache."

"Donnie's being an idiot."

"There's an easy way of testing this," Yates said.

"Please don't make him jump from the roof of the gym."

Donnie frowned. "There's no other buildings close by. I'd be jumping to my death."

"When does jumping become falling?" Ranger asked.

Yates shrugged. "About halfway down, I guess, and as much as watching Donnie jump, then fall to his death would make me feel better, that wasn't what I had in mind."

"Then what?"

Yates pointed down to the mat. "We move these fifteen feet apart, see if Donnie can make it."

"It was more like twenty feet."

Ranger pushed one of the mats away with his foot until he was happy with the distance. He turned to Donnie. "Go on, prove me wrong."

Donnie lifted his chin and marched over to Yates. "Okay then."

He took four backward strides just like he'd done the day before with Elliot, took a deep breath and ran. He launched off the edge of the mat but didn't make the other side. He missed by at least two feet, which made Ranger cheer.

"And that's both your ankles snapped."

"I would've made it."

Ranger pointed at the mats. "You proved you wouldn't have."

"There were different variables."

"Like what?"

Donnie struggled to think of something to say, then blurted, "The wind."

"Oh, the wind again, is it," Ranger said, bowing forward. "Of course, the wind. It would've pushed you across the roof, carried you like a leaf, or are you talking about your own personal wind? You would've launched from the edge like a fucking rocket, gassing the city."

"Adrenaline," Donnie argued. "There's no danger here."

Yates cracked his knuckles. "I can make it dangerous for you if you think that would help."

Donnie backed away from him. "No. I'm just saying, not to mention there was a proper incentive to reach the other side. Elliot was there."

Ranger gestured to himself. "Is proving me wrong not good enough for you?"

"And I've got achy muscles at the moment from charging around the city yesterday."

"You're never going to accept you wouldn't have made it, are you?"

"Nope."

Ranger turned to Yates. "Are you gonna tell him?"

"Huh?"

"Tell him he's wrong, he's stupid, he shouldn't be so careless."

"I'm sure deep down, Donnie knows that."

Ranger darted a look at Donnie, then gave Yates a curious look. "That's a rather measured response from you. I thought you'd be chewing Donnie out for almost breaking his legs. What's wrong?"

Yates sighed. "I'll admit, when you first told me what happened I thought about breaking Donnie's legs myself to teach him a lesson, and to make myself feel better."

Donnie lifted his hand. "I am standing right here."

"I know. Because of Ranger."

Donnie lowered his hand.

"So what is it?" Ranger asked.

"I found out my contacts aren't my contacts…exclusively."

"What?"

"Money doesn't just open doors, but mouths too apparently. Christian's offering a lot of money for information on Elliot's whereabouts, and my contacts thought they'd cash in from both of us. Now I'm in a bidding war for who gets the information first, and Christian is prepared to pay more."

Ranger and Donnie shared a look.

"So what does that mean for us exactly?" Donnie asked.

"It means Christian and his bunch of asswipes will find out where Elliot is before us."

"They'll have a head start."

Yates squeezed the bridge of his nose. "Exactly. They have an advantage over us. This is no longer about money, or Marco. We have to end Elliot to save our reputations."

"We'll get him," Ranger said. "Won't we, Donnie?"

The lump formed in his throat again, the horrible ball of flesh, or tissue, or whatever it was that lodged itself in his windpipe when he needed to speak the most.

Instead of speaking, he nodded, which seemed enough for Yates, but Ranger tilted his head, studying Donnie.

****

Donnie spied Ranger as soon as he walked into the club, as far away as he could get to the speakers, sitting alone. Donnie sighed, waved for his attention, then gestured to the bar.

"Orange juice."

The barman frowned. "You the designated driver or something?"

"No, I just want an orange juice."

Donnie paid for his half pint of orange juice before making his way over to Ranger. Ranger looked at Donnie with the same expression as the barman.

"What?"

"Orange juice?"

"What gave it away, the color?"

Ranger's confusion intensified. "Was the fruit named after the color, or the color after the fruit?"

Donnie groaned as he sat down. "I don't know. I only wanted an orange juice. Didn't realize it came with skepticism and a headache."

Ranger snorted. "It's on the house. Enjoy."

"I try my absolute hardest not to drink, and it seems like the whole world is against me."

"When was your last drink?"

"Three months ago."

"I swear I saw a bottle of whiskey in your apartment last week."

Donnie avoided Ranger's gaze and looked across the club. "So why are we here?"

"Thought we could hang out."

"We spend every other day together at the gym."

Ranger gestured to the dance floor. "Exactly, not here."

Donnie took a sip of orange juice. He needed a level head for the conversation they were about to have anyway.

"Is this about what happened on the roof?"

"Huh?"

"You went…raging."

"It happens."

"What does?"

Ranger turned away. "The red mist—"

"What mist?"

"I couldn't stop it from taking over on the roof. I saw Elliot goad you, knew you were gonna get hurt, and I got so angry—I barely remember what happened after that."

"You almost killed me."

"You kinda deserved it."

"And the red mist?"

"It's gone for now."

"Good."

Ranger pressed his lips into a grim smile.

"You hate…hated clubs," Donnie said.

"I'm trying something new."

"While hiding away in the corner, far away from the dance floor, speakers, and flashing lights."

Donnie yelped when Ranger kicked him under the table.

"I'm meeting someone tonight."

"Oh yeah?"

That was good, Donnie supposed.

"Yeah. Him and his friend will be here soon."

Donnie nodded, then froze. "No way."

"What?"

"This isn't some fucking double-date situation is it?"

"No, of course not. His names Tyler. Thirty. Lives in Trent, works as a bus driver."

"You talking about the guy you're meeting, or the one you're gonna force me to sit with?"

"Don't be like that…and your one."

"For fuck's sake—"

"My one's called Fred. Thirty-three, runs an animal shelter, unless I've mixed them up."

"Great, so not only do I have to make small talk about buses, but I'm gonna go home with fleas, and possibly rabies."

"You owe me."

"Why?"

"For helping get you back into shape, for getting you looking like hot stuff again."

Donnie snorted. "Hot stuff."

"I'm serious. Have you not noticed how many people are looking over?"

Donnie lifted his gaze to the nightclub, then shuffled when he noticed there were people looking over at him.

Not repulsed but smiling. Giving him the look. He hadn't seen that look directed at him for years.

He wasn't even dressed to impress, sporting his worn jeans and his short-sleeved shirt, but heated looks were thrown his way.

"I promise you Tyler's good-looking."

Donnie's headache came back with a vengeance. He sipped his orange juice but grimaced at the bitterness. "I'm not interested."

"Why not?"

"I'm just not."

Ranger didn't blink and didn't look away. He studied Donnie again, like he was trying to work something out.

"Quit staring at me."

"You've been acting weird recently."

"Weirder than drinking myself into oblivion and not knowing what day of the week it is?"

"Not that kind of weird… Weird, weird."

Donnie did bunny ears with his fingers. "Well, I think you're weird for wanting a boyfriend."

Ranger nodded toward the bar, getting Donnie to look. There were two men standing closely together, hand on each other's hips, smiling with loved-up expressions.

"How can you not want that?"

"They're wearing matching shirts."

"It's cute."

"No, Ranger, it's not. They're Hawaiian shirts. Matching Hawaiian shirts."

Ranger laughed. "I think it's cute."

"It's still so strange hearing you talk like that. Admitting you want a boyfriend."

"I think it would be nice, that's all. Someone being there, sex with the added bonus of caring for the person you're screwing, and I even crave doing the normal things."

"Like what?"

Ranger shrugged. "Talking."

"We talk."

"Not about domestic stuff."

"I can come over to yours and complain about the laundry if you want."

"I want to go to the cinema, go for walks, go to the superstore."

"You can do all those things."

"But I don't want to do them alone."

"And what happens if Ranger's Rage is released?"

Donnie had meant it as a light question, but Ranger's face dropped, and he quickly looked away. He pressed his flat hands on the table and looked as if he was giving himself a pep talk.

"Whatever that was, it won't happen. It won't happen again."

Donnie shook his head. "Why is dating suddenly so important?"

Ranger tapped his head. "A few years ago I almost died. I lost all of my memory, woke up in hospital to yours and Yates's ugly faces."

"That's harsh."

"You told me a little bit about who I was, what I did for a job, but it feels so unconnected."

"You loved your job."

"I still do, I think, but there could be improvements, like someone to come home to at the end of the night. Someone other than you two that would notice if I vanished. Someone who'd care if I came through the door bruised and bloodied."

"You've had boyfriends before, you know."

Ranger widened his eyes, then leaned over the table, knocking his drink. Without even looking at it, he caught the glass before it could tip completely.

"What? Who? When?"

Donnie wished he could take back his words, but Ranger was begging for information with his round eyes. It was odd seeing such a big man begging, bobbing up and down, like Donnie held the stars and the moon.

"Tell me about them?"

"I dunno."

"Please."

"I'm not sure that's a good idea."

Ranger had always liked the big, the tattooed, the stare-at-me-too-long-and-I'll-attack-you kind of guy.

"Why isn't it?"

"They were all scary as hell. All huge, intimidating, angry bastards."

Donnie checked around to make sure none were around. Sawyer McQueen had been the worst, a fellow assassin, the worst kind in Donnie's opinion, one that would kill the young, the old, the yet to be born. He had all his teeth replaced with steel ones so he could bite chunks out of people. That was the sort of man that got Ranger's heart thumping and his cock hardening. A psychopath who put Yates and Christian to shame.

"I liked huge and intimidating guys?"

"Yeah."

Donnie drank some more orange juice, hoping the conversation was over.

"How come I didn't end up with Yates?"

Donnie spat out his drink. He wiped his mouth on the back of his arm. "Yates likes his weaker, easy, and paid for in advance."

"That's them," Ranger said, punching Donnie in the shoulder.

The guys coming over looked normal, not insane in the slightest. One tall with black hair and wearing thick-framed glasses, and the other with straw-blond hair, looking ready to bolt. Donnie didn't blame him— he and Ranger looked like giants in comparison, the bone-crushing kind.

Donnie tried his best to offer up a friendly smile, but they were edging closer as if a gun was pressed to their heads. Ranger looked terrifying, always had been terrifying, it was only after the bullet to the head he'd gotten soft, and dare Donnie think it, but shy and tentative too.

He actually saw Ranger wipe his sweaty hand on the back pocket of his jeans before going to greet Tyler and Fred.

Donnie stood up, ready to do the same, but someone caught his eye across the room. The man was leaning against the bar, casual as anything, enjoying his beer. Donnie stared at him, and the weight of his gaze got the man's attention. He looked at Donnie, and Donnie looked back. The rest of the club moved around them; the music blared, the people danced. Ranger growled at him to come over and say hello.

None of it mattered except the man, no longer leaning on the bar but standing up straight. The man with the red hair, the long, crooked nose, and the caught-in-headlights expression.

He ran, and Donnie followed, inevitably knocking Ranger into Tyler or Fred, Donnie didn't know which. Ranger bellowed after him, but Donnie didn't stop to listen.

Hanson Sale.

His botched hit.

Hanson ran for the door.

He burst out on to the street.

Donnie had tunnel vision on his target, knocking people flying as he rushed past. Hanson didn't have the grace Elliot had. His movements were clunky, his footsteps too loud on the pavement, and Donnie could hear him puffing for breath. It wasn't a pretty chase, or a difficult one. Donnie found himself slowing down to prolong it. He'd waited a long time to find Hanson, and he didn't want it to be over before he'd even had a chance to process him being there.

But Hanson was stupid, and instead of running into the crowds, he went for the back streets. Donnie suspected Hanson was confident he could lose Donnie in the maze of alleys, but he'd been training to keep pace with Elliot.

Elliot the fucking eagle.

Donnie cornered him down an alley, pulled out his gun, and before Hanson could plead for his life…

He shot him.

The man that had gotten away a year ago.

The man who had ruined his reputation.

Hanson dropped to his knees, and fell to his side, and the relief that swamped Donnie was so overwhelming he shed a tear. He needed to get out of there before someone came to investigate, but he wanted a moment to breathe it in, except he was at the top of his game once again.

He punched the sky, did a muted cheer, and showboated to an invisible crowd.

He turned to get the hell out of there.

Donnie heard a gurgle, a splutter, then slowly turned back to Hanson.

"I'm still alive, asshole."

"Seriously!" Donnie shouted to the heavens.

He closed his eyes, exhaled a long breath, walking back over to Hanson. "That was a close one—could've fucked it up again. Thanks for being honest about it."

Hanson frowned. "I suddenly wish I hadn't been."

"I really appreciate it."

He aimed the gun at Hanson again, then fired all the rounds in the clip. Hanson went down in a fountain of blood and didn't move, and Donnie took off running as the first siren pierced the air.

He was Donnie—Donnie the comeback King.

CHAPTER ELEVEN

"Hanson Sale," Yates said, pointing at the news headline on his phone. "Found last night, multiple bullet wounds."

Donnie shot Yates a pleased grin. "I did it."

"A year too late."

"Still—"

Ranger quirked his eyebrow. "And five shots?"

"I killed him with the first one but wanted to be sure."

"Yeah. Course you did."

"Stop sulking. I said I'm sorry about doing a runner, but surely you can forgive me. I finally killed Hanson; you knew how much it meant to me."

Yates groaned. "Can't believe you agreed to go on a double date in the first place."

"I didn't agree to it, it was forced on me." Donnie frowned. "How did it go?"

"What, after you knocked me into Felix and I broke his nose?"

"I thought you said his name was Fred."

Ranger shook his head. "Is that all you're gonna say?"

"Look. In the movies that's the moment the hero falls into the love interest's arms, and it's all plain sailing from there."

Yates made a retching noise. "Oh please, spare me the romantic crap. In my movies the hero takes what he wants from multiple love interests, then leaves them full of come."

"That's porn." Donnie laughed

Ranger folded his arms. "I'm two hundred pounds of muscle, and over six foot tall. If I fall on someone, they get crushed."

"No romantic gazing into each other's eyes?"

"Surprisingly no. It's not romantic when his nose is pissing blood everywhere and his friend's trying in vain to beat me away. I got a taxi to the hospital to see how he was but got escorted out by four security guards."

Donnie put his hand over his heart. "I truly am sorry."

"You should be."

Yates put his phone away. "One down, one to go."

"Huh?"

Yates's glare had Donnie retreating a step.

"Elliot, remember?"

"Yeah, I remember."

He pointedly didn't look at Ranger and gestured to the flowers around the shop. They were different, all pastel shades. "How's business?"

"Are you seriously asking me about the flower shop?"

"Yeah, just curious if it's doing well."

"It earns fuck all."

Donnie scratched the back of his head. "Oh, that's a shame."

"Is he high right now?" Yates directed the question at Ranger, then looked at Donnie. "Are you on something?"

"Of course not."

"Didn't have any celebratory drug or cocktail?"

"I'm clean."

"No vibrator up your ass?"

"What the hell?"

"You've got that look about you."

Donnie scrunched his face. "What look is that?"

"Like you're enjoying something, but you're ashamed about it and keeping it a secret."

"I don't have a vibrator up my ass."

"You sure?" Yates asked, looking deadly serious.

"Yes I'm sure! I'm happy I've got Hanson, that's all it is."

Ranger shook his head. "No, you were like this before too."

Donnie threw his hands up. "Like what?"

"Acting all strange and avoiding eye contact."

"I'm not," Donnie said, still not looking Ranger's way.

"What aren't you telling us?" Yates asked.

"There's nothing to tell."

Yates tilted his head, looking Donnie up and down.

"Spread 'em."

"No fucking way. I'm out of here."

Donnie turned to the door, but Yates came at him fast. As soon as Yates grabbed his shoulder, Donnie ducked and twisted around. Yates lost his grip on Donnie, and they squared up to each other. If they came to blows, Donnie knew it would be messy. Six months ago and the fight would've been all Yates, but now Donnie was a contender again.

Donnie was a contender, and Yates knew it.

Donnie readied himself for the first blow, focused on the minute movements of Yates's body as he tried to predict whether he'd punch with his right or opt for his left.

Then there were his feet. Yates could kick like a wild horse. Donnie watched them too, hyperalert to Yates and his weaponized physique. Whatever he chose to do, Donnie was going to retaliate by punching him in the stomach and landing an uppercut to his chin.

Yates snorted, smiled, then backed away.

"It's good to see you're fighting fit again."

Donnie relaxed.

He wagged his finger at Yates. "I'm not spreading my legs for you, or anyone, understand."

"I understand." Yates laughed.

****

Hanson Sale was dead.

Donnie said it out loud to the empty room to help it sink in. It had been two days, but it still didn't feel real.

Hanson was dead, and he still needed to kill Elliot Austin.

Donnie's triumphant smile faded, and he was left staring up at the patterns on his ceiling.

Elliot had outsmarted him at every turn.

Elliot had mocked and teased and humiliated his every attempt.

Elliot, or at least the fantasy of him, had given him a hard-on night after night.

Donnie curled his hands into fists.

He was going to kill him, not only because that was his job, but he had to extinguish whatever lustful fire had started burning.

Donnie shouldn't have craved something from a target, other than their death. He shouldn't have wanted to taste their lips and the rest of their delights.

He shouldn't have wanted them on all fours, with their head turned, panting back at him. He shouldn't have been thinking about it each night, the only cure to the torment jerking off with humiliation and hatred staining his cheeks.

Donnie was going to make Elliot Austin regret mocking and teasing and humiliating him. He was going to make him pay for making him horny and frustrated and damn right conflicted.

Elliot Austin had to die.

Donnie jolted out of his thoughts at the sound of his phone. It vibrated against the glass of water on his bedside table. Six months ago, it wouldn't have been water; it would've been whiskey, or perhaps piss if he'd been feeling too lazy to get up for the bathroom.

Donnie shuffled up in bed, had a sip of water, then grabbed his phone as he sunk back down.

"Little shit," he whispered.

He didn't open the message from Elliot straightaway. He readied himself for it first. He expected a mocking message declaring Donnie was useless, or a picture of Elliot's grinning face while he flicked Donnie the bird, but when he opened it, he frowned at the video file.

It caught him off guard, and he pressed Play without any thought.

Donnie paused the video two seconds in and took a deep breath.

The video was a different kind of taunt.

Donnie's heart was jackhammering after only a couple of seconds of footage. Elliot with his hand wrapped around his cock—that was it, that was all he saw in the two-second clip, but he was damn near hyperventilating, feeling all hot and cold and feverish.

Elliot had sent him a video of himself jerking off.

Donnie gritted his teeth, growling out "little shit" over and over.

He hovered his thumb over the Play button, knowing he shouldn't give in to Elliot's tease. He had already taken so much from Donnie, and when he pressed his thumb down, he knew he was about to take more.

Donnie was going to let him because his hard-on and his curiosity demanded it.

In the clip Elliot moved his hand up and down his cock faster and faster. Donnie couldn't look away, hypnotized by the sight of Elliot's cock. The tops of his thighs, the trimmed fair hair, his cock, blushing pink, a nice size, a nice shape, a nice bead of precome shimmering at the slit.

"Jesus," Donnie breathed.

It was too hot in the bedroom, too stuffy, too restricting. He threw the duvet off himself, and it landed on the floor.

Elliot's breathing hitched, and he stopped his hand.

"Not yet," he murmured.

Donnie groped himself through his boxers, feeling along the outline of his squashed cock until he got to his head. He gave it a squeeze, then growled a curse before slipping his hand inside. His cock was hot and wet, and the neediness of his body filled his face with heat.

Elliot teased himself again, gaining speed before stopping abruptly and muttering, "Not yet, not yet, not yet."

His breathy voice sounded all floaty and blissed. Donnie cursed through his teeth and freed his cock.

Elliot began stroking his cock again, and Donnie matched his pace. He played with himself how Elliot dictated it, until his breathing sounded just as unsettled, just as weak.

Donnie wanted to see his face, wanted to see what it looked like when he gasped in a lustful way, wanted to see him calm down after getting so close to coming. He'd fantasized about it, imagined, but Elliot was so close to showing him, and he wanted to see, wanted to know so badly.

Elliot teased himself until he was close, then crushed his hand around the base of his cock.

"I'm holding on, I'm holding it."

He relaxed his grip, panting.

The external camera flipped to the internal one.

Donnie was gifted with Elliot's pink cheeks, his slightly parted lips and his glazed-over eyes. He didn't look cocky, or smug, just utterly fucked. His eyelashes fluttered, and Donnie knew from all the small twitches on his face and his unfocused gaze he was touching himself again.

"My face or my cock."

Donnie frowned. "Huh?"

"What do you want to see as I come—my cock or my face."

"Cock, face, cock," Donnie groaned, shaking his head.

Both— Donnie wanted both, but he could only see one, and he had no control over it. Elliot had already decided, already finished, and as always, Donnie lagged behind, talking to a video that might have been filmed days before.

"Cock," Elliot moaned, changing the camera.

His cock was shiny and red in his fast-beating hand. Donnie groaned, matching Elliot's rhythm. Donnie rocked his hips, spearing his cock into his hand.

"I want you to fuck me so bad, Donnie."

He wanted that too. As much as he wanted to kill Elliot, he wanted to fuck him. It was messed up, he knew it was, but he didn't stop jerking off to the thought of Elliot on his hands and knees, taking his cock.

"Fucking tease," Donnie groaned.

"Cock or face."

Elliot switched the camera again. His eyes were half-closed, his lips were open wider, and he was making soft little noises that went straight to Donnie's cock.

"I'm so close."

"Come," Donnie growled. "Come, you little shit."

Elliot closed his eyes. "Thinking of you fucking me. Yes, oh fuck."

Donnie panted, waiting for the inevitable. Elliot had made his choice; he was going to give Donnie his blissful face, his pleasure-blown expression. Donnie wanted it so badly, he stared unblinking, wanting desperately to take it all in. He'd be repeating it over and over, but there was only one first time of seeing it.

Elliot whimpered and bit his lip, before gasping, "Bye, baby."

The video ended.

Donnie couldn't believe it. He couldn't fucking believe it, but he was still stroking himself. With the lust came anger, a hateful feeling in his gut both at Elliot and himself. He thought of Elliot's tight lips, tight hole, his near-orgasming cock, and his near-orgasming face, none of which he'd seen at their peak. He'd been teased by the idea but never given it.

Donnie growled through his orgasm, squeezing thick line after thick line of come onto his chest. The red-hot humiliation and anger burned in his cheeks, then fed all through his body, a deep heat of fury.

"Little fucking shit!"

Elliot was playing him, and Donnie was allowing it to happen.

He glared at his spent cock. He shoved it back into his boxers, out of sight. He looked back at the patterns on the ceiling as his heart and lungs settled back to normal and the anger seeped away.

****

Donnie woke to his phone buzzing. He struggled up on his elbows and stared at the dried come on his chest. The phone buzzed by his hip, and he grabbed it. He came close to cracking it in his grip when he saw "Little Shit" flashing on the screen.

"What?"

Elliot whistled. "Someone's cranky. Did you not get my video?"

"Yes I got your video."

"And you didn't like it?"

"No. You're not my type. Didn't even watch it."

"Do you know what I think?"

Donnie collapsed back down on the bed and sighed. "What?"

"You're a liar. I think you're annoyed I didn't let you see me finish."

"Why do that?"

"I like teasing you, like the thought of you getting all frustrated and angry over me."

"You've got a death wish."

"Sure do, baby."

"Why would you send me a video like that?"

Elliot snorted. "That's what couples do in long-distance relationships, right?"

"We're not in a relationship."

"I'm the hit, you're the man. It's a relationship, like it or not."

Donnie scrunched his eyes shut. "This is so messed up."

"Yet here we are, jerking off while thinking of each other, and now this is the post-sex part. Are you a cuddler?"

"No."

"Well, I am, so I'm gonna imagine pressing against you, my head to your chest, listening to your heart. Maybe your fingers stroking my hair, your thumb brushing the side of my face."

Donnie smirked. "You'd like that?"

"Yeah, I would. You touching my head, my face, my hair, and your other arm around me, keeping me in place against your heart. It's warm, and comfy, and nice."

Donnie's heart beat funny, and he couldn't ignore the tickly feeling in his stomach. He pictured what Elliot was saying, and he liked the image painted in his mind. He liked the feeling of calm that came with it.

He shook his head and forced bitterness into his voice. "Sounds disgustingly romantic."

"What's wrong with that?"

"Everything."

Elliot was quiet for a moment, then whispered, "Who was the man on the roof?"

Donnie knew who Elliot was talking about immediately. "Ranger. He's a friend of mine."

"A friend?"

"Yeah."

"He looked like he was trying to kill you."

"He's complicated."

"How?"

"Well, he was worried I was going to hurt myself—"

"So tried to kill you?"

Donnie snorted, and then his amusement died. "He took a bullet to the head a few years ago. He was shot in a superstore, wrong place, wrong time, and he's different to the Ranger from before."

"Kinda like you?"

"No. Not really. I guess his were physical differences that changed his personality. On the roof, the old Ranger came back for a second."

"He was terrifying."

"I handled it."

"I know. If you hadn't had, I would've jumped back over there and tried to get him off you."

"That would've been a foolish thing to do."

"Still would've though."

"I know how to make you come back to me now—pretend I'm in trouble."

Elliot chuckled.

Donnie licked his lips, then murmured, "You have friends?"

"No. Seeing your friend has made me happy I don't have any."

Donnie drew his eyebrows together. "Come on, you must have someone."

"I don't trust anyone. I'm better off on my own."

"You really believe that?"

"Yes. I don't have friends, more…people trying to kill me."

Donnie frowned when the word "people" registered. He was about to ask what he meant, but Elliot spoke first.

"Tell me what's been happening?" Elliot whispered.

"What?"

"That's what I'd ask you if we were still awake snuggling. I'd wanna know what's been happening in Donnie's world."

"My friend tried to kill me, and some little shit keeps winding me up."

Elliot laughed. "You shouldn't let him."

"I'll get my revenge on him one day."

"Apart from the little shit irritating you, and your unhinged friend, what else has happened?"

Donnie frowned. "Are we actually doing this?"

"Yes, we're actually doing this. I don't have friends or anyone to talk to, and I'm feeling kinda lonely, so here we are."

Donnie's stomach twisted. "Fine. I righted a wrong a few days ago."

"Which was?"

"I killed a target that I was supposed to kill a year ago."

"A year ago? What happened?"

"I botched the first attempt." Donnie scrunched his face at the memory, or more accurately, the lack of memory. "I went in boozed up."

"Ah, the whiskey weakness."

"Exactly. He went to ground, disappeared, and my reputation was in tatters."

"But you got him?"

"Yeah. Saw him in the Black Wren, couldn't believe it—"

"The Black Wren in Camden?"

"That's it."

"You were out cruising?"

Donnie narrowed his eyes. "Would you care if I was?"

"I'd like to think we're exclusive during our relationship. The idea of you and others kinda hurts."

"Kinda hurts—Elliot, I'm gonna kill you."

"Maybe, maybe not. I don't wanna be fucked about while we're doing whatever it is we're doing."

Donnie groaned. "This is so messed up."

"You want me—"

"I want. To kill you."

"Small detail—"

"No, it's a massive one."

"Okay, fine, but we both know you want to fuck me too."

Donnie opened his mouth to argue, but his protest died, and he sighed.

"You want me, and I was hoping I'm the only guy you want at the moment. I don't want to be second-best, or your sloppy seconds, or have only half of your attention."

Donnie chewed on his bottom lip. "I wasn't cruising and trust me, you've got my full attention, especially now Hanson's finally dead."

Elliot laughed, not his mocking normal laugh. Donnie thought it sounded more relieved than anything else. "Good. Well done, baby."

Donnie rolled his eyes. "Thank you."

"Bet it feels good, like a weight off your shoulders."

"It does actually."

"How did you do it?"

"I shot him in an alley."

"How cliché."

Donnie laughed.

"Could you not have tried something a bit different—you know, add some flair."

"Like what, attach him to a load of fireworks?"

Elliot whistled. "That would be sweet. You could've dropped him into a tank with a shark or buried him in the ground, covering his face with jelly and let the ants have him."

"These all sound hugely impractical."

"Fun more like. How are you planning on killing me?"

"Might see if the tiger at the local zoo is hungry."

Elliot chuckled, then hummed. "By tiger, I hope you mean you. I'd love you to get your claws into me and eat me up."

"Elliot," Donnie warned.

"What? I would, and I think you'd love doing it too."

Donnie knew that was true. He'd been thinking about it more and more.

"I'm gonna kill you with a knife or gun. How's that sound?"

"Painfully boring."

Donnie snorted. "I prefer the term classic. I'm a classically trained assassin."

"Can I make a request?"

Donnie pinched the bridge of his nose. "I should hang up."

"I'm serious."

"What's the request?"

"If you catch me, I want you to aim for my heart. Gun or knife, it doesn't matter, but the heart, Donnie."

"Elliot."

"Promise me."

The light tone of his voice had gone. He sounded completely serious.

"Fine. I promise."

"Thank you."

Donnie shook his head. "Come on. What's happened in Elliot's world since we last saw each other?"

"I've been laying low, healing up."

Donnie grinned. "Your back still hurting after I floored you?"

"No, brushed that off easily."

"What is it, then?"

"I had a bit a trouble a week ago."

"What do you mean trouble?"

"These three guys were chasing me down and cornered me. I managed to get away, but one caught me with his blade."

Donnie sat bolt upright. "You're hurt?"

"Relax. I'm okay, no need for you to get all territorial boyfriend on me and swear revenge. He got my arm; it's not deep. I've bandaged it up, but that was a struggle on my own."

"You cleaned it first, yeah?"

Elliot chuckled. "Yeah, I cleaned it first."

"And it's definitely not too deep?"

"Barely a cat scratch, baby."

"Can't have you getting an infection and dying, can we."

"Definitely not."

Donnie had a good idea who had targeted Elliot, but he wanted to be sure. "What did they look like?"

"Careful, Donnie. It sounds almost like you care?"

Donnie bit his lip. "I'm only annoyed they've got closer than I have to taking you down."

"Not close enough."

"Are you somewhere safe now?"

"Yes, I've moved. I'm always ready to leave at any moment. My mom was always paranoid, and she taught me well. Starting someplace new is the norm for me."

"And never trusting anyone."

"Yeah, that too."

"It must be exhausting."

"It is, but it's all I've known. I'm feeling rather sleepy now actually."

"Then get some rest."

Elliot yawned. "Will you stroke my hair while I drift off?"

The voice on the other line was so quiet, so soft, it did something funny to Donnie's stomach. He bit his lip, then relented, closing his eyes. "Yes."

"Thank you, baby."

The call ended.

Donnie sunk back down into his mattress while dragging his hands down his face. He wanted to kill Elliot, he wanted to fuck him, and as hard as Donnie tried to deny it, he'd started wanting something else from him too.

The problem was he couldn't have all he wanted from Elliot. He had to choose.

CHAPTER TWELVE

Donnie had spent days thinking about it, but finally, he'd decided what to do. He pushed open the door to the flower shop, poised to tell Yates an unsavory truth, but there was a customer and Donnie was forced to fake interest in the closest flower. A flower that immediately reminded Donnie of a penis. An anthurium—big red flower, and a long ridged "penis" pointing up. He scrunched his toes in his shoes until they hurt when he started thinking of Elliot.

Yates flashed him a blink-and-you'll-miss-it look, then went back to smiling warmly, being the overly muscular flower shop owner with the polite salesman manner. The real Yates wasn't like that to his friends, and certainly not like it to his lovers.

The woman at the counter was chatting with Yates, and by the sounds of it she was a regular from Yates's line of questioning. He asked about her mother, and whether she was still having problems with her dodgy knee. He even used a sorrowful tone when he learned that Philippa was getting a knee replacement. Donnie rather obviously yawned, trying to get Yates's attention. He didn't want to wait; already the prickle of doubt was attacking him.

The woman paid, picked up her pot of purple flowers, then turned around. She stopped when she saw Donnie, but instead of giving him a repulsed look, her lips parted, her cheeks reddened, and she dropped the pot on the floor.

It smashed, and pieces of pot, soil, and plant went everywhere. The woman spun around to Yates, apologizing profusely.

He waved her apology away and laughed. "Grab another one on your way out, Melisa."

"But—"

"It's fine. Let me know when your mother's out of hospital. I want to send her some flowers."

Melisa squeezed past Donnie, and he could practically feel the heat radiating from her cheeks.

"That'll be nice, she'll like that," she said, picking up another pot.

She hurried out the shop, and as soon as they could no longer see her, Yates's amused smile dropped.

"For fuck's sake, Donnie."

"How was that my fault?"

"If you're not terrifying the customers, you're turning them on. That plant's coming out of your share."

Donnie stepped over the pot. "Yeah...about Elliot."

"What about him?"

Yates narrowed his eyes, and Donnie waited for his signature arm cross. His arms folded, pushing out his pectorals, a proper macho pose, as if he dared Donnie to keep speaking.

He swallowed and stopped in front of the counter. "I think I've got a way to track him."

Yates's eyebrows shot up, and his arms relaxed. "How?"

"His phone number?"

"You've got his phone number?"

"Yeah."

Donnie had admitted to one of his unsavory truths, and he could see the cogs of confusion turning in Yates's eyes. It quickly turned into suspicion, and Donnie readied himself for Yates's questions. His sprinkle of truth was about to be guarded by lies.

"How long have you had it?"

"A day."

Yates's arms tightened again, and he went back to glaring at Donnie.

"A day?"

"Yep."

"Where the hell did you get it?"

"That hotel he stayed at, the Fairview Hotel." Donnie gestured to his face. "I managed to sweet-talk the receptionist into telling me the details of his stay. He paid in cash, had no fixed address, but he did supply them with a phone number."

Yates's lips parted. "That's clever, Donnie. I don't know why I didn't think of that."

Before Yates could think too much about it, Donnie handed him a slip of paper.

"Well, here it is."

He'd written it down with a nervous hand, and each misshapen number was a hesitation. Yates didn't comment on his wonky numbering. He gawped at the slip of paper, then shook his head.

"How do you know it's not a fake number?"

"It's not."

"How do ya know?"

"Gut feeling."

Yates hummed. "You haven't called the number, have you?"

Donnie shook his head. "I thought I'd wait to see what you said about it. You're better at this kind of thing than me."

Yates widened his eyes and took a step back. He cleared his throat, then mumbled, "That was wise. You've…you've got your head screwed on."

"Opposed to Ranger, who's got half of his blown off."

"If this is Elliot's number, I'll be able to track him in no time."

"I was hoping so, but I want to go in alone."

"What?"

"He's good at getting away. It's better to have you and Ranger on the outside to close in on him."

Yates rubbed his chin. "Another good idea. Who knew you were capable of them?"

"But I have to be the one that takes him down. He's mine, understand?"

"Yeah, he's yours. Ranger and I both agreed."

"Good. How long until you can find him?"

"I can find where the phone is; no guarantee it's Elliot's though. Will take me an hour or so, enough time for you to get yourself ready and Ranger up to speed."

****

"Can you hear me?"

Yates's voice boomed, and Donnie winced and slapped his hand to his earpiece. "Jesus. Yes, I can hear you."

"I was making sure."

"Try to talk a bit softer, yeah? Lower, so you don't burst my eardrum."

"You want me to use my sexy voice?"

"Christ, no."

Donnie dropped his hand from his ear and shoved it in his pocket. He carried on walking along the path, doing his best to be casual.

"Another two hundred yards or so," Yates muttered.

"I don't see him yet."

Donnie strolled through the park with his hands in his jacket pockets. There were families eating picnics on the grass, some kids running through fountains, others zooming down slides. There were dog walkers and joggers, and an elderly couple sat on a bench watching one tatty duck on a huge pond.

"Is it busy?"

"Yes."

Donnie didn't think he'd seen so many people in all his life. A little bit of sun, and everyone swarmed the grassed areas like locusts.

Yates hummed. "That's not good."

Yates was twenty miles away in the flower shop watching Donnie's tracking dot on a map. He could see the area, could direct Donnie if he had to chase after Elliot, but he couldn't control the people, the witnesses, the Doberman watching Donnie like he was a meal.

Donnie swallowed hard.

"What was that?"

"I saw a mean-looking dog."

"A hundred yards, left of the path."

Donnie frowned, looking ahead. There was no flamboyantly dressed Elliot, no smug smile waiting for him. No man limbering up, preparing to humiliate Donnie all over again like he had by the river, but this wasn't on Elliot's terms.

"I still can't see him."

"Maybe it wasn't his phone number after all."

A group of teenagers on bikes passed by, only narrowly missing Donnie. He resisted the urge to yell after them and instead cursed under his breath.

"What did you call me?" Yates asked.

"Nothing... Wait."

Donnie looked at the bench ahead. There was a couple sitting close together, and on the opposite end of the bench there was a lone figure, dressed in dark clothing, hoodie up and over his head, and stooping forward. His head was low, and Donnie couldn't see his face. When he walked by, the person didn't look up, and they continued staring at the ground.

"You see him?"

"I don't know—"

"You've gone past him according to the map."

Donnie stopped, slowly turned, and walked back the way he'd come. He kept calm, kept casual, and no one in the park reacted or even looked over at his sudden U-turn.

The hooded figure had his hands in his pockets and his feet flat on the ground. Donnie looked at his sneakers. Well-worn and a dulled red color—definitely Elliot's shoes.

It was Elliot, Donnie knew it was, but he couldn't see him properly with how far forward he was leaning, face parallel to the ground, unaware of everything including the couple making out next to him on the bench, and the assassin sneaking closer. Donnie's stomach started to feel queasy. Seeing Elliot like that was odd, like he'd been stripped of all his confidence and cockiness, and that was what remained.

A guy completely alone in a world where everyone else seemed to have someone.

"You see him?"

"Yes," Donnie whispered.

"Easy, Donnie."

He had a gun and a knife but couldn't use either in the crowded park when his face was so visible. There was no pride in being an assassin with your face all over the news. No way to claim your winnings.

Yates seemed to understand his dilemma.

"We went in too eager with this, didn't we?"

"Yeah."

"We know the number's his. Any chance you could get away without him seeing and we can try again? He's got to stay somewhere at night, right?"

"He must be sleeping somewhere."

"Okay, I'd say keep walking, leave the park."

Donnie forced his legs to keep on going, away from Elliot. The unease in his stomach persisted, and his chest tightened as he walked away. He darted a look back at Elliot, still in the exact same position, and Donnie's chest ached.

He wasn't supposed to care Elliot was on his own. He wasn't supposed to care about him looking so unhappy, and small. Every other time Donnie had seen Elliot, his smugness and his confidence had made him seem ten feet tall, but alone on the bench he looked fragile.

It tugged on something in Donnie's chest, and for the first time in months his legs weakened, and he had trouble moving one in front of the other.

"You're a hundred yards away now."

Donnie looked back again, and the tugging and the tightening in his chest hurt. It winded him, so much so he started to exhale slowly, draw a breath in, then exhale it slower.

"That's it, Donnie, nice and easy. Don't do anything irrational."

He shook his head. Yates had no idea.

"Least we've got a way of finding him. I doubt Christian's got hold of his number."

Donnie needed a drink. He needed fifty—being drunk was the only thing that was going to cure him. He didn't know what he was doing anymore, didn't know what he felt either.

A shot rang out, and a scream pierced the air. Donnie spun around to the bench. The man locking lips with his girlfriend pressed down on his gushing thigh while she flapped her hands and screamed for help. Elliot was on the floor, and for a heart-stopping second, Donnie thought he'd been shot too.

"One shot," he reminded himself.

"What?"

"Someone's shooting."

Elliot's wide eyes met his, and he actually looked hurt. Donnie fought back the urge to shout out it wasn't him, he wasn't the one trying to kill Elliot, then quickly remembered yes, he was. There was apparently at least two people in the park that wanted him dead.

Another bullet whizzed through the air, embedding itself into the wooden slats of the bench, closer to where Elliot had curled on the floor. Everyone else in the park ran away from the bench and Elliot, but Donnie crouched and rushed closer.

Elliot seemed dazed, slow to react to the danger, and he stayed curled on his side.

Donnie needed to locate the shooter.

The third shot struck the metal plaque on the bench, and the metallic ping was nauseating in its pitch. The girl pulled her bleeding boyfriend away, somehow still able to scream despite the dead weight she was dragging across the path. She looked at Donnie, and he saw the relief in her watering eyes, but he sprinted past her and she started screaming again.

"Is someone strangling a damn cat?"

There were bushes on the other side of the duck pond, the perfect place for someone to hide and take shots across the park. Donnie unholstered his gun and shot across the pond. He didn't have the range, didn't even know where the man he was trying to kill was hiding, but hoped his erratic shots were enough to stop the gunman from firing for a few vital seconds.

Elliot finally seemed to surface from his sluggish surprise. He took off in a sprint in the opposite direction to Donnie, feet hammering down the path as he tried to make ground before Donnie was out of bullets. He moved with a skilled swiftness, rushing from one tree to another, rolling behind bins and an abandoned stroller. At least Donnie hoped it had been abandoned.

"Can you see the shooter?"

"No, he's on the other side of the pond."

"Then you should be able to see him."

"There's trees and bushes and all sorts."

"Oh, this map's from winter."

"Fucking great."

Donnie rushed for the nearest tree. He skidded along the grass when a shot fired, thankfully no longer at Elliot, but the tree he'd sought refuge behind. He leaned against it and watched as Elliot disappeared into the distance.

"Is Elliot still alive?"

"Yeah, whoever's shooting is after me now."

"Good."

Donnie snorted. "Thanks a bunch."

His earpiece crackled.

"I think it's time the Ranger rounded this asshole up."

Donnie laughed, slapping his clip into his gun. "That would be much appreciated."

"Keep him distracted, Donnie. I'll come up behind him."

"He might have a spotter," Yates said.

"Oh he did," Ranger said cheerfully. "Why do you think I took so long?"

"Distraction, huh?"

"If you'd be so kind, Donnie boy."

Donnie crouched down, placed his gun on the floor, then took his jacket off. He found a well-mauled stick and hooked his jacket over the end. His flailing jacket got the attention of the shooter, and shots shredded the material.

"That was a good jacket," he muttered.

"The Armani one?" Yates asked.

"Yep."

He hummed. "Yeah, that did look good on you."

"Stop flirting," Ranger said. "And he's stopped shooting—make him shoot. Give him something worth shooting, not a damn jacket."

Donnie spied the next tree trunk wide enough for him to hide behind. It was a hundred-yard mad dash.

"Now," Ranger hissed.

Donnie took off, ignoring the whizzing sounds cutting through the air. He skidded the last six feet, getting grass stains all up the side of his leg.

"Did you make it?" Yates asked.

"Yeah, made it. Ranger?"

Ranger didn't reply. Donnie pressed his hand to his earpiece. There were two sets of breathing, two sets of grunts and huffs. A gurgled choking spluttered down the phone before a toe-curling intake of air.

"Shit," Yates said. His voice was perfectly clear compared to the rest of the noise. "Donnie—"

"I'm on it."

He rushed out from behind the tree, scrunched his face up ready to feel the pain of bullets tearing him apart, but no shots were fired. He could hear sirens approaching, knew he didn't have long, and ran toward the pond.

"You better not be dead, Ranger."

He jumped unceremoniously into the water, thought it would be a good shortcut, but he landed in a thick blanket of pond weed. Six months ago and he would've weakened, sank to the bottom, and have been fished out hours later, dead, but he waded through the tangle of greenery, grunting and puffing.

"You got him?" Yates asked.

Donnie gritted his teeth, speaking through them as he attempted to swim. "No, I'm in the pond weed."

"Pond weed? Stop dicking about. Ranger needs you."

Donnie clambered up the other side and yanked his earpiece out. He followed the sounds of rasped breathing and found Ranger being strangled. The shooter had straddled Ranger and had his hands around his throat. He was smirking, completely unaware Donnie had appeared beside him.

He whistled, and the attacker looked over. Long hair, goatee—Donnie realized it was the smirking Greg guy he'd met in the flower shop.

He pulled the trigger, only needing one bullet to sale through Greg's skull. The force of impact knocked him over, and Donnie shoved him in the shoulder to help him all the way.

Ranger wheezed and spluttered, then groaned as he rubbed his throat. He crawled away from Greg, but not before weakly punching him in the side.

"Asshole."

"We gotta get out of here. The police are coming."

Donnie tugged Ranger's shoulder, trying to get him up. Ranger pulled away, cursed, then covered his nose.

"Christ. You stink!"

"That's the first thing you say to me after I've just saved your life?"

Ranger coughed a few times, then grinned. "Yeah, I'm not one for breaking character. You reek so bad my eyes are watering."

"They're watering because he strangled you."

"Whatever."

Donnie shoved his earpiece back in, then instantly regretted it when Yates's harsh tone battered his eardrum.

"What the hell's going on!"

"Ranger's alive."

Ranger shoved in his own dangling earpiece. "Greg and his spotter aren't though."

"Was his spotter Christian?" Yates asked.

"No, I didn't recognize him."

Donnie helped Ranger to his feet. "We've got to get out of here, and fast."

Ranger pointed across the park. "Bike's over there."

"Let's go."

CHAPTER THIRTEEN

Donnie's suit was damp, Ranger was covered in grass stains from his tussle with Greg, but somehow, Yates outdid them both with another monstrosity stretched over his chest. He stood behind the counter in the flower shop wearing a rose-and-leopard-print shirt. He smiled at the customer he was serving, an old man armed with a walking stick and a bunch of geraniums.

He turned around, and Donnie readied himself for his reaction, but even though he and Ranger were a mess, the man walked by without saying anything and left the shop.

"He's blind," Yates said after the bell jingled.

Ranger wrinkled his nose. "Has he got no sense of smell too?"

"Christ, you stink," Yates said, covering his nose.

Donnie looked down at his heavy clothes. Ranger looked at him too, then sidestepped away.

"You really do."

"I can only apologize," Donnie said through his teeth.

Ranger shrugged, then winced and rubbed his throat. Donnie knew it would be days until the bruises showed. Ranger looked his normal self; the only indication he'd almost died was his slightly raspy voice.

"What happened to you?" Yates asked him.

"I got strangled—"

"Yes, I got that part, but you were sneaking up on Greg. What happened?"

Ranger looked away. "I was standing right behind him, about to shoot him, but then I got this intense urge to cut him into pieces."

Donnie's lips popped open. "Right."

"And I didn't know where the sick thought had come from, but it was there, and it distracted me. He turned around and smashed me around the face with his gun. What kind of assassin was I exactly?"

Donnie looked to Yates for help.

At first, Yates had never understood why Donnie wanted to keep the hacking and chopping jobs a secret from Ranger, but years on, even he knew this Ranger was softer, freer, even happier. Yates was a nasty bastard, but not nasty enough to ruin the new Ranger.

He cleared his throat. "A bloody good one."

Ranger narrowed his eyes. "Bloody?"

"At least we know it's actually Elliot's number," Yates said.

Donnie nodded, fully on board with the change in conversation. "And we've taken out Greg and another of his minions."

"How many did he say he had?"

"Five. Christian said there was five of them."

"There could me more. No doubt they'll be after revenge," Yates said. "We're not just after Elliot now, but Christian and his men too. We've got to get them before they get us."

"If Greg's first bullet had hit the target, this would all be over," Ranger mumbled.

The hair on the back of Donnie's neck stood up. "Well, it didn't."

"But if it had."

Donnie didn't want to think about that scenario.

Yates tapped his knuckles on the counter. "How did they know Elliot was in the park?"

"They've been following him best they can."

Yates narrowed his eyes. "And how do you know that?"

"Elliot told me."

"You and Elliot been having little chitchats?" Yates asked, folding his arms.

"Not like that."

That was the truth after all; Donnie just wasn't going to elaborate to a pissed-looking Yates or a curious-looking Ranger.

"He hinted that people were following him that day by the river."

Yates hummed. "I guess it's easier to find him when there's five of them, and they've got my contacts."

"Three of them now," Ranger said, clutching his throat.

"You still tracking Elliot?" Donnie asked.

Yates nodded, then pointed at the shop door. "Ranger, lock it."

Ranger dropped his hand from his throat. "I'm on it."

Yates turned around and led Donnie into the back office. He slipped into his chair, then spun his laptop so they both could see it. Donnie leaned down to see the little red dot flashing on the map.

"He moves quicker on his feet than the cars do around the city."

"You should try chasing him."

"No, thanks. I don't want to be humiliated."

Donnie pointed at the screen. "Where is this?"

"Block of apartments on the rougher side of Barton."

"Isn't all of Barton rough?" Ranger said, closing the door behind him.

Yates snorted. "Point taken."

There were no windows in the small office, and the only light came from the laptop, illuminating all their faces as they stared at the bird's-eye view of Barton. They were all silent for a moment, and the only movement came from Ranger as he continued to rub his throat.

"For fuck's sake," Yates said, yanking open a drawer. He pulled something out, it started humming, then handed it to Ranger.

"The massager will help."

The humming deepened when Ranger put it to his throat. He sighed in pleasure.

"That good?" Yates asked.

"So good."

"Elliot hasn't moved from this spot?" Donnie asked.

"Not for twenty minutes or so. He could be having a rest or—"

"It could be where he's staying." Donnie straightened. "I'm gonna go check it out."

"Not now," Yates said firmly.

"Why not?"

"For one he'll smell you a mile off."

Donnie rolled his eyes. "I'd get changed first."

"Elliot will still be on edge. You need to go in when he lowers his guard."

"Tonight, then," Donnie said.

"Tonight, when Elliot's asleep."

Donnie nodded, taking a step back. He needed a few hours to prepare, mentally and physically. He opened the door to the office, and they all winced at the sudden douse of light.

Donnie gawped at Ranger, then looked down at Yates sitting in his chair.

Yates shot him a wolfish grin.

"What is it?" Ranger asked, snapping looks back and forth between them.

"You're rubbing your throat with a vibrator."

Ranger pulled it away from his neck, pulled a disgusted look, then dropped it. "Yates, you bitch."

"You admitted it felt good."

"That better have been clean."

He nodded. "It is, but if you two don't leave soon, I think I'll get it dirty."

Donnie backed away with his hands up. "We're going. We're going."

"I'll tell you if Elliot moves," Yates said, "If he doesn't, then game on for tonight. We'll finally be able to end this."

"And then there's the small matter of finding Christian and his men," Ranger added.

"Yeah, but that's what tomorrows are for."

****

Barton wasn't a nice place to walk in the daytime, let alone the night. Donnie checked the time on his phone. 23:00. He kept his head low and avoided looking too long at the group of youths on their bikes. He didn't want them to start mouthing off and warn Elliot he was on the way. There was boarded-up shop after boarded-up shop, and an abandoned paper mill at the end of the road.

Donnie stopped, and scanned the block of apartments. Some of the windows were boarded up, and there were fire marks around one.

"This it?"

Static hissed in Donnie's ear, replaced by Yates's voice. "Yes, he's hasn't moved. Apartment 12C."

"You sure?"

"It was rented in the past week. I spoke to the guy—Elliot paid for the room in cash, and he recognized the picture I sent him. I'd say that was pretty conclusive."

"Okay, okay," Donnie said, trying his best to appease Yates. "I didn't mean to offend you."

"I know what I'm doing, Donnie. Now you better know what you're doing. Go in there and kill him."

"What floor?"

"Fifth floor."

Donnie heard voices behind him; the group of young guys were coming closer. Their voices carried, and their lit cigarettes glowed red in the dark. A warning not to linger too long. Donnie was overdressed for a place like that, and if Yates had seen him, he would've ordered him home to change. Suits, hair products, and aftershave were all a foreign entity to the residents of Barton. He'd wanted to look good for Elliot, which was messed up, but knowing that hadn't stopped him trimming his beard or washing his hair or soaping his body up with lime. Donnie would be the last sight Elliot would see, and he wanted it to be a good one.

Donnie stepped casually up the steps, swiftly but silently. He smiled when he didn't hear the slap of his shoes. He didn't need the banister to pull him along and walked with a slight stoop, bending his legs a little to hide from the teenagers below.

Donnie moved just as skillfully along the walkway. He peeked over the side, spying the group of teenagers below. They were quieter than before, but Donnie could still see the faint glows of their cigarettes. If they went out, Donnie would've known they were up to something. Front lights dotted the walkway, but there was no order to them. Some were bright white, some were a dull yellow, and some were out altogether.

Elliot's apartment had a faint yellow light above the door.

The 2 in the number twelve hung upside down, and the C was gone altogether, but Donnie could tell it had been there once from the unpainted shape on the door. He kneeled and peeked a look through the letter box.

"There's a light on in the hallway."

"That's a good sign at least."

Donnie swung his backpack off his back and rooted through to find his lock pick. Unlike the first time he'd tried to break into Elliot's place, Donnie did so with ease. The softest of clunks of the lock sounded like victory, and he grinned at his personal triumph.

"You in?" Yates asked.

"I'm in," Donnie whispered.

He edged the door open, and thankfully it didn't squeak. He placed his feet purposely slowly on the carpet, masking the sound of his movements. Yates was completely silent in his ear, and Donnie knew he wouldn't speak again until he confirmed the job was done or had been botched.

The door to the living space was open, and enough of the light shone into the room to highlight its features to Donnie. It hosted a battered old sofa, a coffee table, and a fridge. All looked ancient, but he could hear the fridge humming, so it at least worked despite being badly dented. There was a half-eaten loaf of bread, a newspaper, and a bottle of whiskey on the side. Donnie recognized the label; although not his favorite, still an enjoyable brand.

Elliot had good taste.

Donnie was about to move on, but his eyes were drawn to the coffee table. There was a piece of paper, and Donnie's heart frosted over. The same thick pen Elliot had used before, except instead of "call me" it read, "Bye, Baby" on a fresh piece of paper.

Donnie stepped closer, lifted the paper, and underneath was Elliot's phone. He hissed under his breath and scrunched the piece of paper into a tight ball.

"What was that?" Yates murmured.

Donnie didn't answer him. He left the room and pushed through the closed door leading to the bedroom. The bed was made, and there was no Elliot snoring softly, no clothes on the floor, and when Donnie rushed into the bathroom, he noticed there was no toothbrush either. He kneeled to check under the bed, then flung open the fragile-looking wardrobe. Donnie hurried back the way he came until he was at the front door. Elliot's shoes weren't there, and his hoodie wasn't hanging on the wonky coat hook.

"Fuck."

"What is it?" Yates asked.

Donnie walked back into the living space. "He's not here."

"Are you sure? His phone—"

"His phone's here, but no clothes, or toothbrush, or shoes."

"Damn it! How did he know we were using the phone?"

"He might have dumped it as a precaution," Donnie said, sinking into the battered sofa. It may have been well-worn, but it was comfortable.

"That kid—"

"Always one step ahead, I know."

Donnie sighed, squeezing the bridge of his nose.

"Back to the drawing board I guess," Yates said somberly.

"Yeah."

"I'll let Ranger know."

The line cut out. Donnie pulled the earpiece out and let it dangle. He still had the scrunched mockery in his hand and unfolded it, staring down at Elliot's words. No hesitation in his lettering, the letters were all big and bold and confident.

"Little shit," Donnie said.

He spread the piece of paper out on the table, grabbed his switchblade from his pocket, and narrowed it to the wood beneath. Donnie took a deep breath to calm himself, then got up, ready to leave.

The whiskey bottled called to him, its amber glow drawing him over like a helpless moth.

He unscrewed the cap, then pressed the bottle top hard against his cupid's bow, taking a deep inhale. Donnie's stomach flipped at the smell, and his heart started to thump. He flung open the cupboards and smiled when there was one clean glass left for him.

He poured himself an unhealthy amount and licked his lips at the sound of it glugging out of the bottle, filling the glass. Donnie pushed the bottle aside, didn't bother putting the lid back on, and snatched up the glass. He left the room, roaming the small apartment again, ending up in the bathroom. He switched the light on, and he stared at himself while its buzz drowned out the sound of the fridge.

Elliot, always one step ahead.

Donnie shook his head and returned to the living room. He pushed the empty glass across the counter until it pinged into the bottle, then braced himself in front of the sink.

He frowned and closed his eyes in a long, hard blink. When he reopened them and stood straight, he swayed. He backed away from the sink and stumbled slightly, before grasping the back of the sofa to stay up right.

"What the hell?"

He swiped his hand down his face, still keeping a tight hold on the sofa.

Something thumped above.

He tilted his head as he peered up at a ceiling panel above the sink. It shook, then vanished, and Donnie blinked at the black rectangle, then gasped as a foot dangled down. A foot with a well-worn red sneaker.

Elliot dropped down, landing on the counter by the sink before hopping to the floor. He had his backpack on his back and looked pleased with himself, his eyes slightly narrowed and his proud grin showing off his perfect teeth.

"I wouldn't let go of the sofa if I was you."

Donnie leaned most of his weight against it. "What…what…" He shook his head before following Elliot's gaze to the bottle on the side.

"The whiskey weakness."

"You drugged me?"

"Hey," Elliot said, "don't go taking the moral high ground. You were gonna kill me."

"But drugging me—it's so…"

"Clever," Elliot said with a twinkle in his eyes. "Easy."

"Cowardly."

Elliot's eyebrows shot up, and then he laughed. "I'm surprised you're still standing; you might want to sit down before you fall down."

Donnie put both hands on the top of the sofa, helping himself around it so he could sit. He tried to keep Elliot in his sights, but it was uncomfortable twisting around to see him, and he gave in and flopped back into the sofa.

"To think I felt sorry for you sitting alone on that bench."

Elliot widened his eyes, shaking his head. "Aww, baby. That's sweet of you. I have to admit it hurt when I thought you'd shot at me."

"I hadn't. Not that time at least."

"I know. You helped me get away."

"Couldn't have that asshole killing you before I could."

Elliot came closer, stepped over Donnie's knees, then sat down on the coffee table. He looked down at the knife pinning his note to the wood, then smirked.

"You gave up my number?"

Donnie swallowed. "I've got to end this."

"Today's not your day."

"I've still got tomorrow."

Elliot swung his backpack off his shoulder and placed it on the floor by the coffee table. He watched Donnie for a long time, then finally asked, "You feeling all heavy Donnie? Like you can't move?"

Donnie flared his nostrils and didn't answer.

"Don't worry, it'll wear off in a few hours when I'm long gone."

Donnie looked away from his gloating face, but Elliot only moved into his eyeline. He didn't just move his head, but his whole body. He crept onto Donnie's lap like a cat and smiled when Donnie didn't grab him. He ran his hands up and down Donnie's sides, finding his gun. Elliot removed it, leaned back, and placed it on the coffee table.

"You're handsome. And you smell..." Elliot pressed his nose to Donnie's neck, taking a deep inhale. "Real good. You wearing that for me?"

He leaned back, taking in Donnie's appearance. "Did you dress up all sexy to kill me?"

Donnie said nothing.

"I'm flattered, Donnie."

He pecked Donnie on the mouth, then smirked.

"Have I made you speechless, baby?" Elliot teased.

He got himself comfortable, then clasped his hands around Donnie's neck, toying with the strands at his nape. Donnie glared at his gloating face, wishing hell on it.

"This reminds me of when we first met."

His eyes were on Donnie's unresponsive lips, his gaze unyielding.

He licked his lips and looked into Donnie's eyes. "I kissed you. You were stunned at first, but then you got angry. I felt it when you kissed me back, the fury that I'd taken your mouth. You kissed me back hard, took over, and I pulled away, ending your illusion of control."

Elliot rested his lips to Donnie's and repeated the words he'd said earlier to Yates. "Always one step ahead."

The words vibrated against Donnie's mouth; the smug twinge sparked a fire. Elliot rubbed his lips against Donnie, and the soft stroke of friction made his stomach fizzle. He kept brushing against Donnie, as if testing him, and then he leaned back and laughed.

"I was struck dumb when I saw you in the park, suited up, gun out, the expression on your face as you pulled the trigger. You're so fucking hot, ya know that, and right here, right now, at my mercy."

Donnie twitched his nostrils, the smallest of movements, but Elliot saw it.

"Don't like that, do you? Being at my mercy, being weak and humiliated."

He leaned in again, and instead of the infuriating rubbing with his lips, he pecked Donnie on the mouth. Once, twice, and then the third time he pressed harder, kissed longer, and when he pulled away, heat sizzled at the wet sound Elliot's lips made. He swallowed, shuffled on Donnie's lap, then went back for another, and another. The wet sounds were going straight to Donnie's cock, and Elliot rubbed against it, circling his hips.

"Do I feel good on your lap?"

The answer was yes. His weight was nice, and his heat burned through Donnie's pants. He could smell Elliot's scent and the hint of Elliot's mouth when he breathed in. The smallest of tastes, but it was intoxicating all the same.

"It feels good to be sitting on it, to be rocking into it."

Elliot slid his hands out from Donnie's neck, stroking his fingers under his jaw before gripping his face hard. He licked his lips, then used his thumbs to lever Donnie's lips apart. As soon as there was a gap, he surged forward, pushing his tongue into Donnie's mouth. He licked leisurely, and although Donnie didn't move his tongue, he still moaned pitifully at the feel of Elliot's tongue, hot and wet, flicking his.

His weakness only spurred Elliot on. He kissed harder, moaning, getting all of Donnie's mouth irritatingly wet. He couldn't wipe the feeling away, and Elliot leaned back, admiring Donnie's puffy wet lips.

"You're hard for me, huh?"

It was obvious. Even though there were layers between them, Donnie could feel the heat at his crotch, not only his, but Elliot's from where he brushed his erection to Donnie's. A firm and lingering greeting between their arousals, controlled by a cocky Elliot. Donnie took a deep breath, trying to keep calm, but it was impossible when Elliot started nibbling at his neck.

"I wanna blow you so bad," Elliot kissed to his throat.

An odd sound escaped Donnie, a moan tapering off into a splutter. Elliot looked at him with blown eyes, breathing fast. His breath was sweet on the air as it brushed Donnie's cheek.

"Do you like the sound of that?"

Donnie thought of Elliot's mouth again, and that led to thoughts of the tight hole he was yet to see. Elliot gave him a quick peck, then asked him again.

"Do you want me to blow you?"

Donnie swallowed another gurgling moan. His cheeks were flaming hot, and the need in his cock scorched.

"Okay," Elliot panted. "Blink once for no, and twice for yes. Do you want me to blow you?"

Donnie blinked twice without pause, then regretted it when he thought Elliot was teasing him some more, drawing out his neediness and adding to the humiliation.

"Again?" Elliot whispered.

Donnie blinked twice again, and Elliot slipped from Donnie's lap, landing on his knees with a thump. He undid the buckle with skillful fingers, then the buttons on Donnie's pants. His breathing was raspy, turned on, and when he freed Donnie's cock, clamminess of Elliot's desperation caressed him before his warm hand.

"Fuck your cock's beautiful," he said with awe, squeezing Donnie's girth.

It felt good, too good.

Elliot curled his fingers around Donnie's cock and started to pump him, experimenting, fast and slow, rolling his thumb on the sensitive seam, touching the head with his fingertips. Rubbing his entire length, tracing his thick veins.

Donnie was in heaven.

Elliot let him go, and that made the fury come back in waves. He flared his nostrils, narrowing his eyes at Elliot, who only chuckled and rolled his eyes. He removed Donnie's shoes, then tugged Donnie's pants and boxers off until he was sitting on the sofa, half-naked. Vulnerable, exposed, his cheeks heated up.

He rubbed Donnie's thighs, squeezing them hard enough to bruise.

Elliot looked good between his legs, massaging his thighs, fixing his lust-blown eyes to Donnie's jolting cock.

Elliot leaned forward, stretching out his long neck, and started to lick.

It was a dream; it couldn't have been real.

Donnie's cock tingled when touched by Elliot's tongue, and he went at it enthused, withering with the need to lick his leakage, to clean him up each time his cockhead got wet. Just like he'd done to Donnie's mouth, he got his cock all wet too, all slippery and swollen. Elliot didn't lick up the wet, he made it more so, until Donnie could feel saliva and precome tickling down the sides of his cock.

Elliot's tongue, his lips, his hot as sin mouth. It threw Donnie into the flames of insanity. His soft moans and groans were answered by Elliot's louder calls, ones that vibrated along his cock and reached even deeper to the base of his spine. Elliot stopped flicking his tongue and lowered his mouth down.

Donnie's breath caught in his chest. Elliot took him deep, and Donnie waited for the moment he gagged and pulled back, but it didn't happen. Elliot was swallowing and sucking, and Donnie could feel the pressure, the heat, the spread of wildfire that told him he was about to come. His cock swelled in Elliot's throat, and he held his breath, ready for the tease to end and for Elliot to give him something, something real, not a tease or a hint or a fantasy.

Elliot pulled back fast, releasing Donnie's cock from his tight mouth. He looked dazed and happy with himself, and the gloating grin came back in force. He darted a look at his backpack by the coffee table, then looked back to Donnie.

He knew what Elliot was about to do. Elliot had worked him up until he was at the tipping point, then planned to leave.

"Bye, baby," he said, wrinkling his nose.

Donnie moved like a striking cobra, the palms of his hands hitting Elliot hard in the chest. He fell back, smile gone, and eyes wide with shock. Donnie followed him to the floor, straddled him, and pressed a hand to the top of his chest, pinning him to the carpet. He stroked himself to completion while anger and triumph blazed in his eyes. His orgasm ripped through him, made more intense by catching Elliot off guard. Come splattered Elliot's face. He had enough time to blink, but his mouth hung open in shock, catching some of Donnie's release.

Once he finished spilling his load, he grabbed Elliot's wrists and pinned his hands to the carpet. He grunted, still too stunned to fight. Donnie stretched Elliot out and kept him pinned with his weight.

He leaned down so they were nose to nose.

"You're not going anywhere, baby."

CHAPTER FOURTEEN

Elliot gazed up at Donnie with wide eyes. He opened his mouth with aborted words, and color filled his cheeks. There was come in his hair and across his popping lips. Donnie could smell his release all over Elliot, and there was no chance of his hard-on going down. A come-splattered Elliot was a perfect-looking one.

Elliot twitched and tried to shake the come off his face. It stayed there, making Donnie grin savagely. Elliot's cheeks were on fire, Donnie could feel the heat.

His embarrassment made Donnie smile wider. He may have been half-naked with his cock smearing on Elliot's abdomen, but he wasn't embarrassed about it. He basked in his own genius.

"You...you drank the whiskey," Elliot gasped.

Donnie scrunched his nose the same way Elliot had when he was about to leave. "No. I poured a glass, walked through the apartment, and tipped it down the sink. I knew you were here somewhere."

Elliot swallowed. "How did you know?"

"Whiskey bottle on the side, one clean glass. Come on, Elliot, give me more credit than that."

"You bastard."

Donnie pouted. "Yeah, one clever bastard who vaulted over your one step ahead."

Elliot's eyes drifted to the side, and Donnie wondered what had caught his attention. The coffee table, the knife, the gun. He looked back down at Elliot and lifted his eyebrow.

"Remember what you promised me?"

"I remember," Donnie said, as cold as ice. "The heart."

"As fucked-up as it is, I'm so glad it's you."

"Why?"

"Because I trust you."

Elliot pressed his lips together until they paled. He scrunched his eyes shut and breathed heavily through his nose, in and out, waiting for it. His breaths got more and more shaky, nervous, and his cock softened in his jeans.

That wouldn't do.

Donnie swung his leg over Elliot so he kneeled one side of him. He readied himself in case Elliot tried to run, but he stayed as he was, boneless on the floor, a lamb to the slaughter.

He pinned both of Elliot's wrists with one hand, then pressed his other to Elliot's chest. The frantic beat of Elliot's heart tickled his palm. Donnie had never felt one go so fast, soft but fast beats like a hummingbird's wings.

"Just do it," Elliot blurted.

Donnie's chest pinched at the plea.

He brushed his hand down Elliot's body, then groped him through his pants. His crotch was still warm, but not hot like it had been when Elliot had grinded into his lap. Donnie wanted it hot again, and hard, and needy enough to go off in Elliot's pants.

Elliot's eyes sprung open, and they found Donnie's, seeking an explanation.

"I'm not done humiliating you yet."

Elliot opened his mouth to speak, but Donnie swallowed his words. He kissed him hard with no negotiation and bullied Elliot's tongue back into his mouth. His kiss was anything but gentle, more a mauling, a brutal takeover. At first Elliot lay limp, letting Donnie get his fill, but then his mouth started to move. His tongue pushed back, and air whistled in and out of his nose. He fought back, and Donnie allowed him a little give and take, let him believe there was some level ground before plunging his tongue deep into his mouth.

He rubbed Elliot's cock and kissed him senseless until heat soaked into his palm, until Elliot's cock was hard and rubbing against his hand, but he didn't stop there.

Donnie kept rubbing and kept kissing even when Elliot started to squirm. His feeble fight back ended with soft moans and splutters and warnings that held no substance. Donnie didn't need Elliot to tell him; he could feel how close he was to coming. His pants were obscenely tented. The heat of his arousal scorched Donnie's palm. Elliot's mouth slackened, loose-lipped and open, soft and for the taking. Donnie slowed his kiss but rubbed faster with his hand.

He licked leisurely into Elliot's mouth, moaning at the taste. Elliot shivered, and his eyes opened for a second, dazed and dark. Donnie leaned in to lick at his mouth, and Elliot's lashes fluttered shut. He whimpered, and the vulnerability in the sound did funny things to Donnie. He lost all control and devoured Elliot's mouth, pressing his palms so hard into Elliot's cloth-covered cock he was certain it was painful.

It didn't matter though. Elliot tensed, gasping around Donnie's tongue. Elliot's cock pulsed, jolting through the fabric.

Donnie pulled back, the sound of their lips losing suction popping in the room. He narrowed his eyes, looking at Elliot with as much scrutiny as he could.

"Did you come in your boxers?"

It wasn't just Elliot's cheeks that were red, but his neck, and his ears too. The humiliation spread like a rash; he could see it as clearly as he could feel Elliot shiver through the aftershocks.

Elliot didn't answer Donnie's question, and he straddled him again, still pinning his wrists, then answered it himself. "You did just come in your boxers."

"Fuck you."

Donnie opened his mouth in mock shock. "Well, that's embarrassing. How did you describe me once?" He pretended to think, then smiled. "Ah, yes. You said I was supposed to be seriously hot, like get an inappropriate hard-on before you die kinda hot. No mention of coming in pants though, that's a first."

"You've had your fun," Elliot snapped. "Now you're being cruel."

Donnie hummed. "I guess it is a bit. Leaving you all dirty like this to be found in the morning. I could clean you up first if you'd like?"

Elliot scrunched his eyes, anger piled on top of his humiliation, and Donnie loved seeing it on his face. The look of outrage while his cheeks still burned and his ears still blushed.

"What the fuck does it matter if I'm dirty or not? I'll be dead."

"But you'll always be remembered for the man that came in his pants because Donnie King was about to kill him."

"I got you hard first, sucked your cock."

"Only because I let you."

Elliot's lips opened, but he had no words.

Donnie wrinkled his nose, lowering his head. "And you felt so good, but I'll never admit that happened. So I'll ask again, do you want me to clean you up first?"

"Yes," Elliot growled through his teeth.

Donnie kept a tight hold of Elliot's wrists and pulled Elliot's pants down with his other hand. He didn't break eye contact and managed to tug them over his ass and down his thighs. It was as far as he could get them in his caged position over Elliot.

The look on Elliot's face was bewildered, confused. Donnie kept looking at his eyes, and he slid his fingers under the elastic of his boxers before forcing them down too.

Elliot swallowed. "I hate you."

"Your cock doesn't. Let's see what I'm working with."

He dragged his gaze from Elliot, to his still-hard cock, sticky and messy. He tutted, shaking his head.

"That won't do. Can't have you found like this, in this sorry state."

Donnie released Elliot's wrists, but he didn't try to reclaim his arms. He'd frozen, frowning and blinking at the ceiling. Donnie shimmied down Elliot's body, then leaned down, nuzzling into Elliot's wetness.

"Donnie," Elliot gasped, and his breathlessness somersaulted Donnie's stomach. "W—what are you doing?"

"Cleaning you up."

He lapped at Elliot's cock, his balls, his sticky thighs where come had stuck to his fine hairs. Donnie hummed as he licked, brushing his hands under Elliot's T-shirt, mapping his athletic body. Elliot tasted good on his tongue, silky like velvet. He pinched a nipple and Elliot gasped.

"You're—you're getting me hard again."

There was shame and confusion in Elliot's voice, and Donnie pitied him and his slow-functioning mind. Donnie flashed his dark eyes up at Elliot, red-cheeked, mouth agape, supporting himself on his forearms so he could watch what Donnie was doing to him. He didn't really think Donnie was going to lick him clean and then kill him, did he?

He gripped the base of Elliot's cock, lifting it nice and straight for him to suck the tip. He didn't break eye contact with Elliot, who went all jittery as if having some kind of spasm. Donnie rubbed his hand up and down while sucking the tip, never losing sight of Elliot's blown eyes. All his other features were marred with confusion, but his eyes showed his want.

Everything was wet and slippery, and he could feel precome on his tongue. More delicate than a release, it was slick, and sweeter. He moaned at the taste, feeling Elliot grow harder between his lips.

Elliot's eyebrows twitched, and his voice was full-on pathetic. "Donnie, I'm gonna—"

Donnie deep-throated him and made the warning a reality. Elliot was coming down his throat, body heaving and thighs trembling. The backs of his sneakers tapped on the floor with the intensity, and then he dropped down, covering his face with his hands.

Donnie let Elliot's spent cock slip from his mouth, and it slapped as it met Elliot's naval.

He tilted his head and stared at Elliot's fingers, waiting for them to part.

"You can't tease me this long and expect me not to fuck with you."

"Fuck with me, or fuck me?" Elliot whispered.

Donnie licked his lips, savoring him. "Both."

Elliot's fingers parted, revealing his black as coal eyes. There was still so much uncertainty and wariness, but Donnie waited patiently. He'd been waiting a long time to have Elliot under him like this. Elliot dropped his hands from his face, then struggled up on his forearms again. His movements were slow, cautious, and he turned his head to take a long look at the coffee table. Knife and gun still exactly as they were. Donnie didn't follow his gaze; he knew exactly what Elliot was looking at. He stayed focused on Elliot so when he turned to him again, their eyes would meet.

They looked at each other for the longest few seconds of Donnie's life. Mouth, then eyes, mouth, then eyes, and then they both moved and pushed their lips together. Elliot battled with Donnie's shirt, and Donnie tried in vain to remove Elliot's T-shirt, but there were too many arms, and it was too hard to do anything when they couldn't stop their mouth-mauling.

Donnie leaned back on his knees, removing his own shirt, and Elliot struggled up to take off his T-shirt. Next were their pants and shoes which they tugged, kicked, and fought off their bodies. Both naked, both panting,

The kissing, nipping, tongue sloshing all started up again, and the hesitation and tension of before dissolved into sounds of pleasure.

Donnie meant it when he said he was going to fuck Elliot, and he tore his lips away to find his pants. Elliot's hands found the back of Donnie's neck. His fingers scratched into Donnie's hair, and he tried to pull Donnie down to carry on kissing. Donnie resisted him until Elliot was hanging off his neck, cursing at him not to stop.

"Lube," Donnie managed.

The magic word in Elliot's world. He released Donnie and dropped to the floor like a lead weight. Donnie scrambled for his pants, finding the lube in his pocket.

Elliot licked his lips. "They said you fuck like a wild thing."

"Not nervous, are you, baby?"

Donnie expected Elliot to narrow his eyes, to swear at him, but instead Elliot swallowed loudly, then murmured so softly it was almost lost, "Maybe a little."

Donnie's insides twisted. Cocky Elliot was momentarily taken over by an unsure one, a younger one. One that made Donnie's heart slow from heaviness. His stomach fizzled again, tingling deep inside.

"I'm not savage, or cruel. If that's what you're worried about."

"Then what?"

"I'm relentless."

"Relentless?" Elliot whispered.

Donnie nodded, leaning down to kiss Elliot. "And selfish."

"Selfish?"

He brushed his nose against Elliot's. "Sure am. I like to take my fill, satisfy myself. You're along for the ride, I'm afraid. It'll be a long one, and I promise you'll enjoy it…at times."

Donnie knew verbal assurances weren't going to sooth Elliot's worry. He kissed him again, then lifted his knees so his feet were flat on the floor. Donnie knew the only way of treating a lover's nerves in this situation was to make them melt.

Donnie moved down between Elliot's legs and got face-to-face with his teasing pink hole. His fantasies didn't do it justice. He gripped onto Elliot's thighs and pressed his face forward. He teased Elliot with his mouth, flicking his tongue, kissing so hard suction popped when he pulled back.

He played with Elliot's cock while he flicked the cap open on the lube, then went back on the attack with his lips and fingers, stretching Elliot open while soothing any rawness with his mouth.

Donnie wasn't lying when he'd told Elliot he was a selfish lover. He did what he wanted, what he loved, and ignored the begging and the pleas from above, and what he loved to do was eat ass. He always bought flavored lube when he knew he was getting some action, and he'd hoped such a moment would arrive between him and Elliot.

Elliot already tasted sweet, but he was licking strawberry out of him, smearing it around his cock and balls, getting him all wet and sticky. Elliot relaxed into it, barely reacting when one finger inside him turned to two, then three. Donnie never stopped licking him, stimulating the bundle of nerves of his rim. He yielded to Donnie's demands, softening for him. He loved the feeling of a tight hole, but a softening one, a submitting one, it drove him crazy with lust.

Elliot squirmed, tossing his head left to right while begging to be fucked. Donnie lifted his head to look at him. His eyes were shut, and his skin glistened with sweat.

Donnie didn't know how long he'd been licking him; he didn't think of time when he was enjoying himself, but could feel the layer of sweat on his body. His hair was damp, sticking to his forehead, and he'd gone at it so long the bottle was used up and the taste and scent of strawberries had long faded.

His hands found Elliot's trembling knees, and he pushed them, encouraging him over onto all fours. Elliot didn't open his eyes but rolled into the right position as if his body was possessed. Elliot offered his well-worked hole, and Donnie guided himself in.

With Elliot's entrance relaxed and welcoming, the best reward was pounding into his ass, gripping his hips, and not stopping until Elliot turned his head to whimper.

Donnie kept going, knew he was hitting the sweet spot by Elliot's fucked-out expression, but it was confirmed for him when Elliot's sphincter tightened, squeezing his cock in an unimaginable tightness. Tighter than when Donnie first started kissing him, Elliot's body gripped onto him, crushing him. He didn't move while Elliot came, just closed his eyes and felt it through their joined bodies.

Elliot gasped wetly, collapsing forward. Donnie gripped his hips hard enough to leave marks and tugged him back up, pulling Elliot's lax body to him, making his body fuck itself on Donnie's cock. He pulled Elliot onto him over and over again, loving the smooth glide he'd created.

He grunted, unsatisfied, and slipped out of Elliot's hole. He stood up, then yanked a boneless Elliot to his feet. Donnie tugged him into the kitchen, encouraged him to lean over the counter, then started fucking him again with earnest. He wanted Elliot in every room, their sweat and come everywhere, a trail of their fucking and Elliot's downfall.

Donnie loved to fuck, had iron control and a thirst that was hard to satisfy. He'd lost his libido after his deadly mistake, but Elliot had rekindled his desires. He couldn't get enough of rocking into him and listening to the sound of slapping flesh and gasping. His cock tingled with the suggestion of orgasm, but he wasn't ready for it yet, and he forced it back.

He changed position and location again, had Elliot folded over on the floor in the hallway, and pistoned into him. Elliot let himself be had, never fighting Donnie. Sweat dripped down his face, down his neck, and Donnie couldn't resist drinking that up too. Missionary on the kitchen floor, followed by Elliot on top while he sat on the sofa. Elliot only managed a few bounces, before weakening and letting Donnie take over, driving up into him until dribble left the corner of his mouth and he barely clung on to consciousness.

Donnie finished in the bedroom with Elliot on all fours on the floor. He plunged deep, dug his nails into Elliot's hips, and let the orgasm finally steal him. He couldn't breathe, could only tremble and wait for his cock to stop spilling before taking in a vital breath.

Donnie sat down on the edge of the bed, pulling Elliot down on top of him. Elliot shuddered and tucked his nose under Donnie's damp chin.

"I think you've got one more in you, baby," Donnie cooed.

Elliot knocked his head to Donnie's throat, out of his mind. "I can't."

"Yes you can. I want you to, so you will."

Elliot whimpered, all frail and exhausted, and Donnie kissed the side of his neck. He pressed his palm firmly into Elliot's lower stomach, making circling movements, hoping to torment his squished prostate. It seemed to work: Elliot shuddered, releasing a wrecked moan, and his cock started to stiffen again. It didn't harden to the point it had when they'd first started, but enough for Donnie to work with, enough to make him come.

"That's it." Donnie kissed into his neck. "Come for me, Elliot."

When he did, it didn't shoot out, it dribbled from the tip, covering the back of Donnie's fingers. The sound that left Elliot was relief with a hint of pleasure, opposite to how they'd started. Donnie smirked, then stopped toying with Elliot's stomach and cock.

The hours of fucking Elliot caught up and slammed into him like a truck. He eased Elliot off, gripped him under the shoulders, then threw him on the bed. He bounced on the mattress and stared up in a daze.

"I think you've killed me."

Donnie collapsed next to him, utterly exhausted but finally satisfied. "No. Not yet."

CHAPTER FIFTEEN

Donnie's eyelids were weighted, but he forced them open and reached across the bed to Elliot. He pawed at air, still dozy, but when he realized Elliot was gone, his heart rate rocketed. Elliot had disappeared while he slept, snuck away from him in the night.

The toilet flushed behind him. The bathroom door squeaked on its hinges, and then a set of heavy footsteps plodded closer. Donnie pretended to be asleep, listening to Elliot, wondering what he was about to do. Elliot got to the edge of the bed, crawled over Donnie, then burrowed under the duvet. Donnie settled back down, watching Elliot fondly as he rubbed his head on his pillow.

"I thought you might run," Donnie whispered.

Elliot snorted. "Don't think I'm gonna be running for a while."

"Sore?"

"A bit, and achy, and..."

"And what?"

"So fucking tired."

Elliot had left the bathroom light on and the door open. Donnie could see him clearly. The exhaustion under his eyes, his matted-with-come hair, the utter defeat in his face. Donnie reached out and touched his cheek. Elliot pressed into Donnie's hand and sighed.

"I'm tired, Donnie."

"I know."

When the duvet slipped from Elliot's bicep, Donnie saw the slice in his flesh just as clear. It stole his attention from Elliot's eyes. In his lust he hadn't noticed the cut, but in the calm of the bed he saw it, and it made him unexplainably angry.

"What did the guy look like that did that to you?"

Elliot quirked his eyebrow. "Gonna go all territorial boyfriend on me?"

"Tell me."

"Everywhere I went, they seemed to be there, looking for me. They cornered me, I managed to get away, but the guy stabbed me. I don't remember much about what he looked like; I know he had long hair though—whipped me in the face when I struggled past."

"A goatee?"

"I think so."

"He was the one shooting at you in the park. I killed him."

Elliot widened his eyes. "What?"

"I shot him at point-blank."

"Yeah?"

Donnie nodded. "Yeah."

"I guess that's kinda nice to hear." Elliot smiled. "Sure you don't have a territorial streak?"

Donnie laughed.

Elliot reached for Donnie's arm and ran his fingertips along the scar by his elbow. "How did you do this?"

"Ran into a burning building to save some kittens."

Elliot chuckled. "Oh yeah?"

"Yeah, saved them, then blew the flames out with a single breath, easy as that."

"Did you kiss the girl too?"

"Her and her mother."

Elliot cracked another laugh, and Donnie couldn't help but smile at him.

"I'd like to say I burned my arm doing something heroic, but I think I leaned on the stove when I was wasted. I've got a few scars like that, too drunk to know where they've come from."

Elliot frowned, as if considering Donnie's words, and then he stretched out his arm, showing Donnie a silvery line that went from his wrist to his elbow.

"How did you do that?" Donnie whispered.

"I was too cocky; thought I could make a jump that I couldn't. Ended up going through a window and slit my arm open."

"You getting in trouble for being overly cocky…that's a shocker."

"I've got a few like that, my overconfidence being my downfall."

"Where are the others?"

"You can't learn all my secrets in one night. There would be no reason to keep me alive in the morning."

"Why parkour?"

"It's freeing. I feel almost…"

A blush hit Elliot's cheeks, and he shook his head.

"Tell me."

"No."

"Please."

"I felt—I feel superhuman, uncatchable, unstoppable, and when I asked people to film me, they were always amazed, in awe, and I guess it felt kinda good when people looked at me like that, like I was something worth watching."

"You are infuriatingly good."

"I've never managed moving vehicles though."

"That sounds awfully dangerous."

"It is, but you've seen the movies, right. Jumping from a bridge onto a moving train."

"They're movies. In real life they'd be splattered like a bug."

"Maybe. A few times I tried, stood on a bridge willing myself to jump, but couldn't."

"I'm glad you didn't."

Elliot grinned. "So why a hit man?"

"It pays good—one hit a year supports you as long as you don't overspend. I was good at it. Ruthless, stylish. I guess I liked people being in awe of me too. I liked being good at something."

"You still are."

"I'm lying in bed with you, not killing you."

Elliot hummed, then pulled his pillow out from under his head. He shoved it on his face, and grabbed Donnie's wrist, leading him to the pillow to smother him.

Donnie snorted, flipped the pillow up, then kissed Elliot on the mouth. Elliot's lips stretch into a grin beneath his, then pulled away.

"Yeah, I think you've gone soft if you're kissing instead of killing."

Donnie slipped his hand beneath the duvet again and pulled Elliot onto his side. He could feel his ribs, knew Elliot was skinnier than when they'd first met, and was hit by a sudden pang of guilt. He'd been hunting Elliot down like a dog the past few months, barely allowing him a breather, and Christian and his men had been added to the mix too.

"Why do you never go far?"

"Huh?"

"You stay in the city—it's a big city, granted—but with that money you could leave here, get on a plane, start somewhere new."

"I liked the idea of winding up my dad, popping up here and there in the city he runs. He can't get rid of me, no matter how badly he wants me gone. At least that was the reason at first."

"And now?"

Elliot shot Donnie a look before looking away just as quick. "Maybe I like you coming after me. Maybe I was afraid if I strayed too far you wouldn't come. Maybe I actually quite like you, Donnie."

"You're crazier than I thought."

Elliot snorted, then yawned. "I'm sleepy."

He looked at Donnie, then shimmied closer. Donnie rolled onto his back, and Elliot's head ended up on his chest, resting there. He hesitated a moment, then started stroking Elliot's hair, careful of the clumps he couldn't work his fingers through. Elliot let out a contented sigh, and Donnie sunk into the bed, feeling relaxed, a sense of peace landing over him like a blanket.

Elliot sprawled over him felt good—more than good.

Elliot didn't speak again, and his breathing leveled out. Donnie played with the hair at Elliot's nape, twisting and untwisting the strands, careful not to tug too hard or sharply.

Elliot didn't trust anyone but had somehow formed an attachment to Donnie of all people, a man sent to kill him. Elliot said he trusted him, and Donnie didn't know why, but that trust was a nice feeling no matter how misplaced.

Elliot was lonely, had a warped idea of being wanted, and had found some kind of solace with Donnie, but more messed up than Elliot's attachment to him was his attachment to Elliot. He wasn't supposed to care, or feel sympathy, or desire, or anything for his marks. He was supposed to kill them at the first opportunity and collect the money, but Elliot pulled on something deep in his chest, something he couldn't escape from.

Donnie closed his eyes and played with Elliot's hair for as long as he could before falling asleep too.

****

Elliot escaped the bed again while Donnie was sleeping. He stiffened, then relaxed again when the shower began hissing in the bathroom. He swung his legs out of bed, stretched, then opened the bathroom door to find Elliot. The humidity slapped Donnie in the face, and he blinked to adjust to the steam. He spied Elliot's backpack, and his toothbrush and toothpaste by the sink.

Elliot tugged the shower curtain open. "Don't even think about coming near my ass."

"I won't come near it—I'll come in it."

Elliot shook his head, then pulled the curtain back across. Donnie grabbed Elliot's toothbrush off the side and cleaned his teeth, all while the shower masked what he was doing. When he finished, he slipped into the shower, barely enough room for both of them, and pressed his front to Elliot's back.

"I mean it, no touching my ass or cock."

"Your mouth though, that's still up for grabs, right?"

"Maybe."

Donnie grabbed Elliot's chin and turned his head into a kiss. Elliot spun around and slipped his arms around Donnie's neck.

Elliot sighed when he pulled away, then rested their foreheads together.

"What the hell are we doing?"

Elliot voiced what Donnie was thinking, but he couldn't answer. He didn't quite know but didn't want to stop. Instead of answering the bigger question, he answered the simple one.

"We're kissing."

Elliot snorted, then slipped his tongue into Donnie's mouth. Their tongue swirls were leisurely, accompanied by nose sighs of contentment and a slow rocking movement of their bodies. The hiss of the shower and the heat all around them let Donnie drift away and enjoy the kiss. It felt as comfortable as the calm that had come over them the night before. Donnie had never had a kiss that good, a slip and slide that felt somehow familiar but was completely new.

Elliot pulled away, then narrowed his eyes. "You used my toothbrush, didn't you?"

"Would you have preferred me not doing my teeth before kissing you?"

"Okay, fine."

"You snuck out of bed again."

"Your snoring woke me up," Elliot said, lifting his chin. "And I needed to get the come off me."

"Kinda liked it on you."

"Pervert."

Donnie gripped Elliot's face. "Me dripping down your chin, like you said I would."

"I am rather consistent."

Donnie smiled, then leaned closer to press their mouths together. Elliot opened his lips immediately, wanting a deeper kiss, and Donnie was more than happy to oblige. He wrapped his arms around him, feeling the water rush down his back. He couldn't resist groping Elliot's pert ass as they locked lips, but Elliot slapped his chest.

"No ass or cock action."

"Sorry," Donnie muttered without an ounce of sincerity.

"And I'm hungry. I'll fix us some breakfast."

He tried to leave the shower, but Donnie grabbed his wrist. "How do I know you're not gonna run?"

"I never run on an empty stomach."

Donnie rolled his eyes.

"You're gonna have to trust me. Trust me or put a bullet in me right now."

"Now there's an ultimatum."

He eased his grip on Elliot's wrist, then huffed and released him altogether. Elliot got out of the shower and dried himself while Donnie watched. He washed his hair and body in record time, got out of the shower, dried, then went to hunt down Elliot.

He stepped into the living room, and Elliot swung a frying pan his way. He ducked instinctively, glaring at Elliot as he lost himself in manic laughter.

"Couldn't resist."

Donnie yanked it from his hand and put it on the side. "How about I get us something to eat?"

"You want to cook for me?"

"Want is a strong word."

Donnie kept Elliot in his sights as he found his clothes on the floor. Elliot picked up his backpack and tugged it open. He pulled out a plain white T-shirt, boxers, pants, and socks.

"No peacock-print shirt?" Donnie asked, raising an eyebrow.

"Did you like that? I wanted to make sure I stood out in a crowd."

"Most people try to keep a low profile."

Elliot shrugged. "When I found out it was you trying to kill me, it sounded more fun than anything else."

"Because you thought I'd never be able to."

"Yeah."

"And now?"

Elliot looked at the coffee table again, but Donnie didn't follow his gaze. He knew what was there, completely untouched. His loaded gun and drawn knife. Elliot looked back at Donnie and tilted his head.

"I think you could. You're capable of killing me now, but you won't."

"Isn't it that overconfidence that had you slicing your arm open?"

"If you were going to kill me, you would've done it by now."

Donnie finished getting dressed. "I don't kill on an empty stomach."

His phone buzzed in his jacket pocket, but he ignored it. He had no idea how he was going to explain to Yates what was going on with Elliot. He didn't even know himself.

"You not gonna answer tha—"

"Breakfast," Donnie said, clapping his hands. "What have you got?"

"Bread, and I think there's some cheese in the fridge."

"Grilled cheese is it, then."

Donnie tried to keep Elliot in his field of vision, but it was impossible. He grabbed the cheese out of the fridge, then whipped around to make sure Elliot was still there. He did the same manic twirl with the bread, and Elliot smirked.

"I mean it, I won't run on an empty stomach."

"And I won't kill on one."

"Looks like we've got a truce."

"Yeah…for now."

Donnie's phone buzzed again, but he ignored it, shot a cautious look at Elliot, then turned his back on him to make the grilled cheese. It didn't take long to prepare their meagre breakfast, and they sat side by side on the sofa with their thighs touching.

"You make a good grilled cheese," Elliot said, brushing crumbs off his T-shirt.

"I think anything tastes good when you're ravenous."

"True."

"I'm sorry I couldn't make you pancakes."

Elliot slowed his chewing, then swallowed. "How do you know I like pancakes?"

"You know…when I shot at you in that pancake place."

"When you killed the owner, you mean?"

"Yeah, that. You like pancakes."

Elliot bobbed his head. "And you want to cook me something I like because…?"

Donnie exhaled slowly. "No idea. This whole thing's confusing. I feel more confused than when I was downing a bottle of whiskey every day."

"I heard the owner was a dirty old man. I'm glad you killed him."

"Thanks, but I wasn't actually aiming for him."

Donnie's phone vibrated his thigh again, the thigh rested against Elliot. He looked down at their shaking legs. "So you gonna answer that?"

"I guess I should."

Yates would've known he'd stayed at the apartment—he was tracking Donnie after all—but Donnie didn't know if he was ready to explain why he was still there, and why Elliot was with him, alive and leaning heavily into his side.

He shot Elliot an apologetic look, got a hand between them, then pulled out his phone. He'd expected Yates, but Ranger's name flashed on his screen. Thirty-three missed calls from Ranger and double the number of messages. Before he had a chance to read one, the phone buzzed in his hand.

Donnie answered and put it to his ear.

"Why the fuck haven't you been answering!"

Elliot shuffled away from him, and he shifted away from Elliot, leaving a gap between them.

"I—"

"I should hack you into pieces while you're goddamn alive. In fact, I might—next time I see you, you'd better run. I'm gonna take your pretty face apart slowly."

Donnie's lips parted in shock, and for a moment he didn't know quite what to say. Ranger wasn't himself again, or he was himself again depending on how Donnie wanted to look at it.

"Ranger—"

"Thirty-four goddamn calls, Donnie."

"I know. I was busy."

"Busy doing what?"

Donnie flashed a look at Elliot. He didn't answer Ranger and expected more threats down the phone, but instead slow breaths fizzled like static, and he suspected Ranger was trying to calm himself down.

"Are you still thinking about cutting me up?"

"No," Ranger mumbled. "I needed to know you were all right."

"I'm fine. What's happened?"

"Some guys came to my place last night, tried to kill me."

"What— Are you okay?"

"Yeah. There was two of them. I thought I was a goner—they trapped me in the kitchen away from my gun, but I saw the knives, and well, I don't remember much else."

"Raging Ranger."

"Yeah, it got pretty messy. I think Christian sent them, and that's not all."

Donnie pinched the bridge of his nose. "What else?"

"Yates's shop got set on fire last night, and I can't find him anywhere. I've checked the hospital, his place, his usual go-tos, but he's not there. They've only just put the flames out. The building isn't safe to go inside yet. I think he might be—"

"Don't say it," Donnie said, getting to his feet. "I was talking to him last night. He can't be." He shook his head. "No, no way."

"If he was okay, he would've contacted one of us."

"I don't believe it; I can't—there's no way."

But he knew Ranger was right. Yates would've suspected Christian and got in touch with him and Ranger to bring him down.

"Where are you?" Ranger asked.

Donnie ran his hand through his hair and turned back to Elliot. When his big blue eyes met Donnie's, his chest tightened to the point he could barely breathe.

"Donnie?"

"I'm at Elliot's apartment."

"Why? You went there last night. Yates sent me a message saying Elliot wasn't there."

Donnie winced; he had no idea how Ranger was going to react. There was a chance he'd still pursue Elliot for the 200K, and they'd be forced to face off against each other.

"He is here, with me."

"What the fuck, Donnie?"

"The thing is…I can't kill him."

Elliot gave him a small smile, and Donnie swore his eyes looked wetter.

"What does that mean?" Ranger asked.

Donnie scrunched up his face, and Elliot frowned. "Well, technically, I can kill him."

Elliot's lips parted, and he dragged his backpack closer with his foot.

"What I mean is, I won't kill him," Donnie finished. "I won't stab him, or shoot him, or do anything to hurt him."

"Why the hell not?"

"I just won't, and I won't let anyone else do it either."

"Is that you warning me off?"

"Not specifically you, but yeah, I'm warning everybody off him."

Elliot looked so goddamn happy, Donnie's eyes started to sting. Ranger was quiet for a long time, then huffed.

"Okay. I guess we're not killing Elliot, then."

Donnie breathed out in a rush. "No. We're not."

"We've still got Christian and his men to worry about though. If they went after me and Yates last night, they probably paid your place a visit too. Is there anyone suspicious lurking around?"

"It's Barton," Donnie answered. "Everyone's suspicious."

"Valid point, but is anyone acting more suspicious than usual?"

Donnie pointed at Elliot. "Stay there."

He tore his gaze from Elliot and left the room. He opened the front door, stepped outside into the sunlight, and looked down on the road below.

Donnie frowned when he saw a group of youths on bikes. Couldn't tell if they were the same ones from the night before, but they were definitely looking up at the apartments. Donnie's gaze snapped to one of their backpacks, bright green. Two blacked-out SUVs drove up the road, and one of the teenagers waved them closer.

"Shit," Donnie hissed, going back into the apartment.

"What is it?" Ranger asked.

"I think this place is being watched."

He rushed back into the living room where Elliot was obediently waiting.

"Or more accurately, I think Elliot's being watched."

Elliot's lips popped open, and a line appeared at the top of his nose. "What?"

"Yesterday at the park, there was group of teenagers on bikes. I remember because one nearly knocked me down."

Elliot shook his head. "I didn't notice them."

"Well, they're outside right now, and they've got company."

"Have they seen you?" Ranger asked.

"Yeah."

He sucked in air. "Shit. I'll get there as quick as I can."

"Okay," Donnie said.

The line went dead. Donnie leaned down, gripped Elliot's wrists, then pulled him to his feet. He fell into Donnie's chest, blinking up at him.

"You better be ready to run."

Elliot bit his lip, then nodded. "And you better be ready to kill."

CHAPTER SIXTEEN

Donnie flung open the door to the apartment, then walked in a crouch toward the stairwell. He couldn't see the cars below from his position, but voices carried over, then the slam of car doors. Donnie darted a look behind to see Elliot leave the apartment. He didn't duck or crouch; he ran straight out and bolted in the other direction, away from the stairs. He was the bait after all, the nice dangling prize that Donnie hoped would make the idiots below overlook any danger.

"There he is!"

Donnie kept still and silent and listened to the slap of feet on the stairs. The huffs and puffs and in one case growl of the men rushing the steps. He aimed his gun, and as soon as the first man popped his head around the corner, he pulled the trigger. It hit him in the head, and blood sprayed into the air like water from a sprinkler, then he fell back, landing with a thud.

"Shit!"

Donnie kept quiet. He listened to the men on the stairwell. He slipped down a few steps, careful not to make any noise, gun at the ready, body poised.

"That Donnie King was with the kid."

"Christian wants us to kill him too."

"Go on, then."

"You go."

Donnie sighed. "Come on, one of you, we don't have all day…"

"Why don't you come down here?"

"Careful what you wish for."

He launched forward, one shot, then another, before the two men even had a chance to lift their weapons. More blood, more dull thumps as one hit the ground, and the other tumbled back down the steps he'd just rushed up.

Donnie slipped down the next set of stairs, holding his breath, but he didn't hear anyone rushing up to meet him. He peeked a look over the wall at the street below. The teenagers had gone, and only one blacked-out car remained.

Donnie turned at a static hissing coming from the dead man who'd taken a tumble. He went back to him, flipped him over, then unhooked his radio.

"Elliot's going into the paper mill."

"Surround it."

It sounded like Christian's voice; Donnie was sure of it.

Donnie stared down at the body at his feet while clutching the radio. He'd seen the paper mill; there were no buildings around it. Elliot would be trapped.

He saw a figure in the dead man's glasses, a man creeping up on him, or more accurately a giant. He rolled to the side, spun around, but the man grabbed his gun, managing to push him away as he fired.

At least two hundred and fifty pounds, bigger than Ranger and Yates put together. He straddled Donnie, and he tried to flip him off, roll him over, but he was too heavy. The man's fist came toward him as heavy and hard as a dumbbell, and Donnie's head smacked into the concrete floor. He tried to sort his muddled mind, fend off the dizziness, but he whirled as each fist pummeled him into a state of near unconsciousness. His cheek split, his lip burst, and at least one tooth rattled around in his mouth.

Donnie's vision spun as he was elbowed in the head, then knocked in the chin. There was a sudden chill to his palm, and he realized at some point in his beating he'd lost his weapon. Another punch landed on Donnie's face, and blood ran down from his nose. He had to get off the ground, knew he was at a massive disadvantage with the man on top of him, punching him while he couldn't move far enough away, but everything was feeling off, detached.

He saw Yates's face in front of him, floating there, and the memory of his voice. "That all you got?"

That was what he'd kept saying to Donnie at the gym, then on the mats when they sparred together, Yates doing his best to get him ready for moments like this.

Yates and Ranger had both worked hard to get him job-ready again, and Elliot needed him. He couldn't lie there and take it.

His spiraling brain snapped into focus.

Donnie managed to get his forearms in front of his face. A fist came down on him, and Donnie opened his arms enough for it to come close, then clamped his arms around the man's wrist hard. He managed to twist and hurl the giant of a man off him before dishing out his own hand-to-hand beating.

He didn't hit with his fists, but the palms of his hands, over and over, as fast and brutal as he could until the man's nose broke and his face streamed with blood.

"Had enough now, huh?" Donnie asked.

The man grumbled, then spat blood in Donnie's face.

"Thought so."

He grabbed his switchblade from his pocket, then stabbed the giant right in the chest. He held the knife there, wriggling it inside his body, slicing up his heart until he relaxed of all tension.

Donnie collapsed on the floor next to him, panting away the pain in his face. He was dribbling blood, and he frowned at the mess he was making on the floor, then reached for the small cube of white. He squeezed his tooth between his fingers, searching with his tongue to find where it was missing.

One of his top molars.

Donnie flicked it away, grabbed his gun, and got shakily to his feet. He snatched up the radio, then rushed down the stairs.

Blood dripped down from Donnie's eyebrow. He struggled out of his jacket, then used it to mop up his face. His cheeks felt overly tight, and the swelling pressed on his sinuses, making it uncomfortable to breathe.

The delivery truck was parked at the corner of the street, not Donnie's normal go-to vehicle, but it was rumbling away with the driver gawping out of the window with his phone to his ear. He dropped his phone as soon as he saw Donnie running toward him and held up his hands.

"I don't want any trouble."

"Get out the truck, then."

The man opened the door and tumbled to the ground. Donnie stepped over him and climbed into the driver's seat. He tossed the radio on the seat next to him, then put the truck into drive.

"He's on the roof."

Elliot's go-to place for escaping, except the paper mill stood alone. Donnie pulled off from the curb and put his foot down.

He could see a silhouette on the edge of the building, knew only Elliot would stand that close to a deadly drop. Donnie punched the horn on the truck, getting Elliot's attention.

Donnie smashed the truck into the cars that were parked by the side of the paper mill, knocking them away so he could get as close to the building as he could. He couldn't see Elliot, could only hope that he was watching above, could see the truck parallel to the building, only a few feet between them.

Donnie saw the end of the building, and his heart squeezed thinking Elliot had missed his chance. He'd be gunned down on the roof and Donnie wouldn't be able to get there in time to stop it.

There was a loud thump on top of the truck, followed by a quieter one. Donnie steered back onto the road, praying Elliot had landed on him, and that he was okay.

He checked the mirrors, and there wasn't a body on the road behind him. Whoever had landed on him was still there, conscious, or unconscious, he didn't know.

Donnie winced at another thump on the roof and leaned over to open the passenger window.

Elliot's worn red trainers dangled down, and then he slipped through the open window as if it was the easiest thing in the world. The relief that swamped Donnie was so intense he almost crashed into a lamppost, managing to pull the truck onto the road at the last second.

"Did you see that!"

He didn't sound hurt, or afraid, but elated.

Donnie smiled. "Sadly I missed it, but I heard it."

"I jumped onto a moving truck."

Donnie snorted. "Not as impressive as a train though."

"Screw you."

Elliot's gleeful face dropped when he turned to Donnie. "Jesus."

"I know. Got pummeled by a giant and lost a tooth. I'll clean myself up as soon as we get somewhere safe—"

"It's not that."

"Then what?"

"Didn't think you could look any sexier, but there you are, cuts and slices and blood."

"What?"

He shot a quick look at Elliot, then looked again. Elliot heaved for breath. His hair stuck up everywhere, and his eyes were so wide and black he looked like he'd taken something.

"You've seen me bloody before—frying pan, remember."

"Yeah, but..." Elliot gestured to Donnie—the reinvented Donnie. "And this wasn't done by me; it was done for me so I could get away...you took a beating for me."

"I prefer to think of it as I killed three people for you."

Elliot's lips parted. "Three. You killed three people for me..."

His voice was so soft, a wisp of sound Donnie wasn't sure was meant for his ears.

"For me?"

"Yeah...and me as well, but mainly for you."

Elliot looked down at the floor of the truck, still gaping.

"Elliot?"

His head snapped up, and he pounced across the seat at Donnie, getting into his lap. He started kissing his face, over his dribbling cheek, his split eyebrow, and his stinging lip. It hurt, but each painful peck filled Donnie's chest with something nice, something warm and relaxing.

Donnie tried to keep his head tilted to the side, eyes on the road, but Elliot grinded into his lap with a fevered desperation, and he could already feel the effects. His groin hardened at Elliot's stroking, and the need to kiss Elliot into submission rose until he started trying to kiss back. Elliot kept moving, and he growled in frustration before remembering they were in the middle of getting away.

"Gonna crash."

"Sorry, sorry," Elliot said, easing his onslaught. "I'm just…very…happy right now."

He leaned back, looking at Donnie, waiting for him to look back. The road was straight and clear ahead. Donnie shifted his gaze to Elliot and his big blue eyes. The eyes that burned Donnie right in the heart. He kept one hand on the wheel and cupped Elliot's face. He leaned into the touch and closed his eyes, and the moment of sudden calm was serene and blissful.

"Good."

There was a smash of metal, and Donnie was thrown forward, crushing Elliot into the steering wheel. Something had slammed into them hard. Donnie saw the SUV in his mirror, coming up behind them. It careened away, then drove back hard into the side of the truck.

"Put your seat belt on," Donnie ordered.

Elliot clambered back into the passenger seat, put his belt on, then leaned over to clip Donnie's belt across him. The SUV hit them again, and the back wheels of the truck spun out, moving them from side to side. Donnie fought with the wheel, trying to keep the truck under control. He battled against oversteer and understeer as the truck screeched down the road. Donnie managed to level out the truck, but the car trailing them was relentless and knocked them again and again.

The truck tilted. Donnie couldn't get it back down on all of its wheels, and he knew it was going over. He gritted his teeth as it fell, wincing as it slammed into the road. The sound was near deafening, a horrible metallic scraping that brought back memories of twisted metal, of helplessness and regret. He saw sparks on the road, orange lines dancing, threatening something bigger, something deadlier, and he looked at Elliot squeezing his eyes shut.

When the truck came to a stop, he gripped Elliot's shoulder and shook him gently.

"You okay?"

Elliot was holding on to his seat belt so tight, his hands were trembling. He opened his eyes and took a shaky breath.

"Yeah."

They'd fallen on Elliot's side of the truck. The glass from his window had gone, and all they could see was a square of road.

Donnie unclipped his belt, careful not to land on Elliot. They shifted around in the cab until they were both standing up right. Donnie kicked the shattered windshield until it came away completely and crumpled to the road. He ducked down, and Elliot did the same.

They hadn't even made it out of Barton yet, had landed farther up near another apartment block. There was a green in front of it, a few trees that attempted to make the place look nice, but that was impossible when there was a burned-out car behind it and graffiti that told the residents to eat shit and die.

"Go," he shouted.

Elliot looked at him with wide eyes. "What?"

"Run, get away. Now. I'll be right behind you."

CHAPTER SEVENTEEN

Elliot escaped the truck first, but Donnie was hot on his heels, gun drawn, firing shots to cover their getaway. Donnie heard voices, car doors slamming. There had been four men in the other SUV, and Donnie predicted there were four in the one that had tipped his truck.

A bullet pinged off a trash can, another thumped into a tree. Donnie ducked behind it, then peeked a look out. He could see the black SUV and all of its doors open, five men crouching as they ran toward him.

"Wonder which one was squished in the middle."

Donnie jumped at Elliot's voice. He was hidden behind a trash can, a few feet from Donnie.

"Get out of here."

"I wanna see you do your thing."

The men were fanning out. He had barely any cover from the tree. "Shit."

"What?"

"We're too exposed here."

Elliot hummed. "You're right. I'll lead those three off, you sort the other two out."

"What?"

Elliot took off before Donnie could protest. The three men on Donnie's right changed direction and went after Elliot. He was sure one of them was Christian.

Elliot had left him with two, and he needed to dispose of them as quickly as possible.

Donnie took out one of the men with a skilled headshot, grinned, went to shoot the other, but he was all out. He didn't have another clip or more bullets. He hadn't imagined he'd be in a shootout when he paid Elliot a visit.

"Shit," Donnie hissed, making a mad dash for the burned-out car.

Shots peppered the ground, flinging up earth. Donnie skidded behind the car, but not before a bullet grazed his arm. He grunted, clutching the wound. He was lucky it had only skimmed the surface, but it wasn't pretty.

He opened the car door for some extra cover before crawling into the footwell. He needed his assailant to come close enough for him to use his knife. He was shooting the car, and Donnie thought he was safe until a bullet zinged straight through the metalwork, close to his head.

Donnie frowned at an engine's roar.

The firing stopped.

He looked up in time to see a bike thunder across the green. The rider had one hand on the bike, one hand on a minigun. He tore up the man in a hail of bullets and blood before skidding to a stop in front of the burned-out car, every bit the action hero.

"What's happening, bitches."

Donnie groaned, rolling out of the car. "I'm all out."

Ranger lifted his shades into his hair. "Funny, would've said you were all in."

"I meant my gun's all out. How did you find me?"

"Tracked your phone."

Donnie stumbled up and rested his hand on the car for support.

"We've got to get Elliot."

"Which way did he go?"

Donnie pointed at the apartment block he'd seen Elliot rush behind. "That way."

"Then climb aboard."

The bike wheel reared up, and Donnie cursed and gripped onto Ranger hard. They shot between the buildings and in the distance could see figures running. The sound of the bike made them stop and take up positions.

"Ranger, I'm out. It's on you."

"The thing is, Donnie, I'm out too."

"What!"

"But they don't know that."

Ranger controlled the bike with one hand and aimed the minigun with the other. Donnie thought what the hell and held out his gun too. No one dared poke their heads up or fire back. Ranger made bullet spray noises under his breath, and despite the peril and the impending doom, Donnie still laughed, and like two kids they made the sounds for their guns, pretending to shoot.

They rode past Christian's men to the fire escape Elliot was rushing up.

"Who's that after him?"

Ranger pulled up beside it, and Donnie jumped off the back. He ran up the first set of steps with Ranger behind him. "Looks like that Nigel guy."

"The guy that refused to shake my hand."

"Yeah?"

"I can't stand rudeness."

Donnie attacked the next set of stairs. Ranger's feet clipped the back of his heels.

"Oh the irony."

"What?"

"You used to be the rudest bastard of them all."

They hit the top of the roof in time to see Elliot jump the gap to the next building. Nigel didn't stop; he ran and jumped too, landing on the other side.

"You gotta be shitting me," Ranger hissed. "Don't you dare think about it."

Donnie sprinted out of Ranger's grip, got to the edge of the building, and leapt. He made the other side, but his victory was short-lived when he fell too far forward, landing on the heels of his hands and grazing the hell out of them.

"You're an idiot!" Ranger shouted.

"Thank you," Donnie growled through his teeth.

"But a goddamn handsome one."

Donnie climbed to his feet and avoided looking at his hands. He could feel them stinging, could smell the blood, but he didn't want to see them too. He hurried after Nigel and Elliot and saw when they got to the bottom of the fire escape. Elliot ran, but Nigel caught him and tackled him to the ground.

Nigel recovered faster than Elliot. He got to his feet, went to shoot, but Donnie threw his knife just in time. It somersaulted through the air, then stabbed straight through Nigel's eye. He dropped to his knees, then fell forward, pushing the blade farther into his head.

Elliot panted up at him on the stairwell. "That was the coolest thing I've ever seen."

"You've got to go," Donnie said.

Elliot met him on the bottom step and shook his head.

"We've got to go."

Donnie looked back for Ranger but couldn't see any sign of him. "Come on, then, along here."

He led Elliot between the buildings, but they were trapped by a padlocked gate.

"We'll find another way."

Elliot rolled his eyes. "Or we just go over it."

Elliot made climbing over a gate look like a fine art. He landed on the other side, then bowed.

"Your turn."

Donnie shook his head. "This is the perfect time for you to get away."

"So, what, you're sending me away?"

"I'm telling you to go so that I can find you again once this is all over."

"You promise?"

"I promise. Trust me."

"I do."

Elliot gestured Donnie closer.

"There's no time."

Even as he said the words, he moved to the fence. Gaze trained on the end of the alley, ready to protect Elliot at any cost. His gun was gone. His knife was in someone's head. He only had his fists that were busted and bloody, and his body that he'd use as a shield if Elliot needed it.

"Donnie," Elliot whispered.

Donnie flashed a look at Elliot behind the fence. His fingers were clutching the wire, and he shook it so it rattled so Donnie would look again.

Elliot smiled at him, a look so devastating Donnie lowered his guard and ignored his instincts. Elliot pressed his face to the wire, lifting his chin, opening his lips in a clear invitation he wanted to be kissed. Donnie rocked on his heels, caught in two minds. He gave in and pressed his face back hard, capturing Elliot's mouth.

Elliot didn't fight Donnie for the lead. He was soft and coaxing with his tongue and let Donnie take his mouth exactly how he wanted to. It was bloody, and it stung. He could smell blood and sweat, but it was utterly perfect.

Elliot smirked, and Donnie pulled away.

He checked no one was approaching from behind them, then asked, "What?"

Elliot let go of the wire and walked backward away from Donnie. He licked his lips, groaned, then winked. Donnie knew what he was about to say before his lips had even begun to move.

"Bye—"

Elliot twisted so violently it robbed Donnie of the ability to speak. Blood sprayed from his side, and the sound of the shot registered in Donnie's ears. The pip was as devasting as the car exploding that haunted Donnie's dreams, and the same helplessness, self-disgust, and guilt hit him.

Elliot crashed to the ground, clutching the trickling wound. The shot hadn't come from behind Donnie, but behind Elliot.

Christian Black.

Elliot dragged himself behind a dumpster out of sight of Christian. Donnie curled his hands around the wire, glaring Christian down.

Christian's eyes blazed pure fury, and his hand was unshaking on his gun.

"You and that brain-dead one have killed shitloads of my men."

"They were trying to kill us, and we retaliated."

"We got Yates though—incinerated in his precious flower shop."

Donnie flared his nostrils but didn't move.

"Are you still broken?" Christian said. "This is where you turn and run."

"You'd just pop me in the back."

"Yeah, I probably would."

Donnie started to climb the fence and was surprised when Christian let him. He clambered over the top, landing on his hands and knees on the other side. He didn't have the grace Elliot had, and expected him to chuckle, but Elliot's face was stark white, and he shook his head, seemingly wishing Donnie hadn't done that.

"What you planning on doing?" Christian asked.

"Doing?"

"You're Donnie King, the best—surely you've got something up your sleeve."

Donnie lifted his arm and his scraps of sleeve hung down, all dripping red. "I don't."

Christian circled Donnie, frowning. "You've got nothing to kill me with?"

"That's not why I climbed the fence."

He backed away from Christian, then crouched down to reach for Elliot.

"What the hell are you doing?" Elliot said, trying to push him away.

Donnie sat down with him. He leaned his back on the wall, pulling Elliot close.

Elliot hissed, then growled through his teeth. Not a fierce growl, but a wounded one. Donnie's stomach knotted when he pressed his hand to Elliot's wound. Thick blood ran through his fingers.

"I'm staying right here."

He said the words to Christian, but it was a promise to Elliot.

Elliot stopped trying to push him away and instead pressed his head to Donnie's chest, burying his face in his heart. Donnie's beat calmly despite the fact he was staring down the barrel of a gun.

Christian snorted. "I've got to hand it to you, Donnie, it's kinda brave facing death like this. Consider your pride restored, in my eyes at least."

"Get on with it."

Donnie brushed his fingers into Elliot's sweaty hair, cradling him as they waited for their end. Beneath the smell of blood and sweat, he could smell the shower gel Elliot had used that morning, minty and fresh. They were pressed so tightly together he couldn't tell whether it was his own warmth. Elliot was breathing against his chest, hot little breaths that heated and cooled with each inhale and exhale.

Donnie frowned at the grumble of an engine, not Ranger's bike, but something else. It came closer, and Christian scrunched his face, looking toward the mouth of the alley. Donnie couldn't see it from behind the dumpster, but Christian's eyes widened, and his lips parted in a silent scream.

The sound got louder, and the wall vibrated, rattling Donnie's spine. Christian shot at the car, but it didn't have any effect. The car went straight into him, and straight through the gate. Christian flipped into the air, his limbs twirling like he was a ballerina, before crashing back down to the ground. He landed in front of Donnie and Elliot, a tangle of broken parts, but to be sure, the car reversed over him.

Donnie gawped at the car. Elliot escaped his chest to see what had happened. Ranger popped his head out the passenger window on the opposite side to Donnie. He looked over the top of the car at him, covered in blood, grinning ear to ear.

"What's happening, bitches!"

Donnie's gaze didn't linger on Ranger. He found Yates.

Yates in the driver's seat, looking furious.

"I don't have all day," he snapped.

Donnie nodded dumbly, then lifted Elliot off the floor. He managed to get Elliot onto the back seat, then jumped in after him. Ranger was smiling brightly at him from the front seat, but Yates just scowled through the mirror.

Yates, who had the stomach-turning aroma of burned flesh.

There were blisters on his face and on the back of his hands, and Donnie coughed at the soot coming off him.

"I got out of the shop just in time," Yates said.

"You don't say…"

"He's off his face on drugs to deal with the pain," Ranger said.

"That's not exactly comforting."

"I got myself sorted out, then tracked your phone."

Elliot tugged on Donnie's shirt, and he looked down. "Why can I smell a BBQ?"

Ranger burst out laughing.

"It's nothing for you to worry about," Donnie promised. "You concentrate on staying alive, you hear me?"

Elliot gripped the back of Donnie's neck. It was weak; Donnie could barely feel it. He was deathly pale and kept blinking, trying his best to focus on Donnie when his eyes kept drifting to the side.

"You would've died with me?"

Donnie nodded. "No question about it."

"That's so romantic," Ranger sighed.

Yates shifted in his seat. "Makes me sick."

"Your smell makes me sick."

"Do you want me to throw you out of the car?"

Donnie smiled fondly, stroking Elliot's pale cheek. It was strangely comforting hearing Yates and Ranger bicker while watching Elliot's frown deepen, trying to make sense of them in the front seat.

"Who the fuck are they?"

Donnie laughed. "Friends that were helping me kill you."

"Now we're helping to save you," Ranger said.

Yates snorted. "And we use the term 'friends' loosely."

"You're assassins too?" Elliot asked.

"Yeah."

"You're all shit at your job."

Ranger burst out laughing, punching his seat. "I like this kid."

"He's mine, back off."

"I would say I'd fight you for him, but I actually think you might win."

Donnie grinned, looking down at Elliot. He ran his finger down Elliot's nose, before tapping the tip. "Course I would. I'd fight the world for him and win every time because he's goddamn worth it."

Elliot's hand slipped from his neck. "This sucks."

"That's not supposed to suck. It's supposed to be nice."

"It is. It's so fucking nice," Elliot whispered. "I wish I'd met you sooner."

"We met when we were supposed to meet."

Yates hissed from the front seat. "Oh please—"

"Shut up," Ranger said firmly.

Elliot shivered. "I'm so tired, Donnie."

"We're gonna get you to hospital. They'll fix you up. Then you can run for me to follow."

Elliot's face crumpled with pain, and he shook his head. His eyes were teary, and his bottom lip wobbled. Donnie stroked along it, easing its trembles while shushing Elliot.

"It's okay. You're gonna be all right."

"I said you'd never catch me."

Donnie tightened his arm around Elliot's back just enough for him to feel. "I have got you, haven't I?"

"I'm gonna run where you can't follow."

A tear landed on Elliot's cheek, and Donnie realized it was his own. Elliot felt cold and clammy against him, all except the hole in his side Donnie had his hand over. Blood pressed against his palm, and as Elliot battled to say more, Donnie saw the blood in his mouth staining his teeth.

"You're staying right here, with me, understand?"

Elliot looked up at him with fear and pain. There was a flicker of something in his blue eyes. Donnie frowned. He'd seen that look before—mischief.

Elliot's lips lifted into a lopsided smile. His blue eyes lost moisture onto his lashes, and then he murmured, "Bye, baby."

He chuckled, smiling his teeth-flashing smile.

All red and wrong.

His eyes lost their focus on Donnie, and he stared at the roof of the car.

Donnie shook him. "You little shit. Don't you dare."

Elliot blinked slowly, then closed his eyes. His smile faded, and a slow sigh breezed past his bloodied lips. Donnie shook him again, but there was no reaction. Elliot was completely still in his arms.

"I can't—I can't without you. You saved me. Please hang on and let me save you too."

There was no answer from Elliot, and silence from the front seats.

CHAPTER EIGHTEEN

Ranger closed his hand around Donnie's shoulder, giving him a gentle squeeze. He didn't turn to him; his eyes were locked on the very dead-looking Elliot in front of him.

His pale skin was uncomfortable to look at, the blue hint to his lips stomach-twisting, and the blood trail leaking out of him was too much to bear, but Donnie didn't look away. The horrible image burned into his mind, leaving a forever print of Donnie's worst nightmare.

Elliot dead—there was nothing worse.

"And you're all done," Yates mumbled, slipping his phone into his pocket.

Elliot opened his eyes and blinked up at them. "Yeah?"

He was lying on the floor of Donnie's apartment. They'd pushed all the furniture away to make a big blank space, then put makeup on Elliot to make him look dead. The worst part was the blood, real pigs' blood, running from a prosthetic gunshot wound.

"Who knew a Halloween prosthetic could look so real," Ranger said.

Donnie nodded. "Disturbingly real."

"Yes, very authentic-looking," Yates said.

Donnie huffed. "A little too authentic if you ask me."

"It's got to look real, okay. Your boy toy is fine."

"Boy toy." Donnie snorted. He looked at Yates; the scarring to his face was minimal, and Ranger was already on at him to turn them into a tattoo, a rose on his cheek to remind him of his flower shop.

Elliot jumped to his feet, swayed, then clutched onto his side. He hissed through a wave of pain, and Donnie steadied him.

"You're supposed to be taking it easy."

"I'm fine."

Donnie slipped his hand beneath the bottom of Elliot's T-shirt, finding the scar with gentle fingers. Not the bullet hole, but the surgeon's scar where he'd cut into Elliot to save his life.

Elliot was down a spleen, but still had his life.

"Hopefully that will convince Marco," Yates said.

Ranger nodded. "Or he'll hunt us down like dogs."

"I'll send it to him in a few days once you've left the city, then transfer your share of the 200K."

"I think me and Donnie should take fifty percent," Elliot said, lifting his chin toward Yates.

"And I think you should keep your trap shut."

"I almost died."

Yates pointed at the ground where Elliot had been laying moments before. "You're supposed to be dead. It's only because Donnie's dick's interested in you that you're not."

"Fifty percent."

"Your death can still go ahead if you're gonna be a bitch about it."

"Not happening," Donnie said, tugging Elliot closer.

"Ranger and I could take you."

Ranger scrunched his face and raised his hand. "Actually, I'm with Elliot and Donnie on this one."

"What?"

"The lovebirds need money to set up home somewhere."

Yates made a retching noise. "I can't stomach much more of this sweet-ass bullshit."

Ranger smiled at Donnie. "I for one can. I can't wait to find myself the one."

Heat hit Donnie's cheeks. "The one? That's a bit too fairy-tale romance for me."

He yelped when Elliot pinched his side.

"Am I not the one?"

"The one that got away repeatedly, maybe. The one that humiliated me, infuriated me, sure. The one I couldn't kill, the one I won't kill, and I'll die protecting, completely."

Ranger pointed his finger. "The one that you wept like a kid over when you thought we were too late to save him."

Donnie narrowed his eyes. "Asshole."

"Aww, baby," Elliot said, gripping Donnie's face. "You cried for me?"

Yates nodded. "Not only cried, he was screaming his head off. My ears were practically bleeding by the time we got to the hospital. Thought the doctor was gonna have to sedate him, wailing down the corridor after you like a fucking banshee."

Elliot wrinkled his nose. "How embarrassing."

"I thought I'd lost you," Donnie protested. "I was devastated. It's romantic, right."

He looked at Ranger for support, but he only held his hand out, indicating 50/50.

"Screw you all."

Elliot tugged on Donnie's neck to get a kiss. One that Donnie gave while narrowing his eyes. "It was sweet of you crying and shouting after me, but there's a thing called dignity."

A rumbling laugh escaped Yates. "Oh, he gave his dignity up to me months ago."

Ranger snapped his fingers for Elliot's attention. "You wanna know embarrassing? Donnie once crawled across the floor to kiss Yates's shoes. He wanted a job that badly."

"No way," Elliot said.

Ranger nodded frantically, and Yates laughed. Elliot looked at Donnie, and he saw the twinkle of mischief in his eyes.

"Think I can top that."

"How?" Ranger asked.

"When Donnie was chasing me down in the mall, he tried to run up the wrong side of the escalator but wasn't fast enough. Ended up jogging on the spot in front of everyone looking like an idiot."

"That's fucking brilliant," Ranger said.

Yates chuckled. "Might see if I can find that footage."

"If you do, send it to me, yeah?" Elliot said.

"I think it's time Ranger and Yates were leaving," Donnie said, then looked at Elliot. "And you need a shower, I can smell that blood."

"Why did we even have to use pigs' blood?"

Donnie wrinkled his nose. "Yates said it comes out better in the photos, looks real, isn't that right?"

Yates shot Donnie his sinister smile.

"You were bullshitting, weren't you?"

"I wanted to see how gullible you are. Very, apparently."

Donnie groaned. "Get out of my apartment, or I'll throw you out."

Yates turned to leave. "With pleasure."

"Wait...thank you." He looked back and forth between Yates and Ranger. "Both of you, for saving Elliot, and saving me."

"Someone had to," Yates said.

"I owe you."

"I'm sure I'll think of some way you can repay me, but for now, we're done. I would say it was nice to meet you, Elliot, but it wasn't."

Yates turned around and left the door open behind him.

"He's grumpy at the best of times, but I don't think he could handle any more public displays of affection," Donnie said.

Ranger tilted his head. "One day, when he least expects it, I'm sure he'll find himself someone, or someone will find him."

"I have so much sympathy for that person already."

"Yep, me too."

"Keep giving that dating app a go. You'll get lucky, I'm sure of it."

"As long as I can keep Raging Ranger under control…"

"I'm sure you will."

Ranger averted his gaze. "Anyway, I'll leave you to shower and have sex. Can I make a suggestion?"

"You're gonna make one whether I want to hear it or not…"

"Have sex in the shower—then there's less mess."

Elliot laughed. "Very good suggestion."

Ranger beamed at him. "Right, I'm going. Have fun."

He squeezed Donnie's shoulder, then left the apartment, closing the door softly behind him.

"Shower?" Elliot asked.

Donnie nodded. "I'll meet you in there. I've got to clean this up first."

He gestured to the blood on the floor, not Elliot's blood, but enough of a reminder that Donnie was uncomfortable with it there.

Elliot slipped from his arms. "Okay."

Once he could no longer see Elliot, Donnie rushed into the kitchen for some wipes to clean the floor. Only when it was gone did he feel better again. Even though he knew it was fake, seeing Elliot like that had gotten to him. It made him think of the ride to the hospital, all his unanswered pleas, and the times he shook Elliot and there was no response.

Donnie shook the memory away and went after Elliot.

Elliot whistled as he washed his hair. The scent of lemons filled the room, and Donnie undressed while watching Elliot's blurry outline.

Donnie climbed into the shower, coming up behind Elliot. Elliot sagged into him, leaning most of his weight onto Donnie's chest. He reached past Elliot and placed a bottle of lube on the side, a clear indication of what he had planned.

Elliot chuckled. It was only just audible above the spray, but it made Donnie smile. He gripped Elliot's hip with one hand and wrapped his other around his abdomen, careful of his scar. It had been four weeks since his operation, and although Elliot seemed to think he was back to normal, Donnie knew he had to be careful with him.

He ducked his head and started kissing the side of Elliot's neck. They were openmouthed kisses, and he sucked water droplets from his skin before licking over the patches with his tongue. Elliot moaned, then moved his head for Donnie to caress the other side of his neck.

Donnie touched with his teeth, not biting but scoring. Elliot shivered and pressed his palms on the tiles to support himself.

Donnie relaxed his grip on Elliot's hip and slipped his hand lower, slower than the water running down Elliot's body.

"Don't tease me."

"I'll do as I please," Donnie mumbled behind Elliot's ear.

He touched Elliot's cock, only fingertips at first, feeling the length and hardness. Elliot was eager for him, eager for his touch. He took hold of Elliot and started rubbing.

"Yes!"

He smacked his head back into Donnie's chest, unintentionally giving Donnie more access to his neck. He sucked Elliot's skin, not hard enough to bring blood to the surface, but hard enough to make him quiver down to his knees.

Donnie picked up the pace. He looked at the bottom of the shower cubicle and smiled at Elliot's toes, scrunching up on his restless feet. He muttered under his breath; Donnie pressed the side of his head to Elliot's to hear him. He kissed his cheek when he realized he was encouraging Donnie, chanting at Donnie not to stop.

"Only for a minute, baby."

He let go of Elliot's cock and reached for the bottle of lube.

Elliot cursed, pressing his forehead to the tiles. He stuck his ass out, arching his back. Donnie ran his hand down it, then slipped a well-lubed finger along Elliot's crack. Donnie tested the flesh with his fingertip, touching the outer rim. Elliot groaned like an animal and rocked his hips forward, and Donnie answered his call with a groan of his own.

"Fuck me."

Donnie leaned down to bite Elliot's shoulder. "Patience."

"But—"

Donnie spread Elliot's legs wider, then returned his fingers to Elliot's ass, stretching him open, adding more lube. Elliot's restraint softened, until he was only capable of moaning and rocking his hips back to swallow Donnie's fingers.

"If it's too much or hurts, tell me."

"It hurts that you're still talking and not fucking me."

Donnie chuckled, then positioned his cock at Elliot's entrance. He wrapped his arms around Elliot, then started flexing his hips. His thrusts were cautious and slow, and he closed his eyes at the sensation of feeling Elliot. He was taking what he wanted, fulfilling his desire, and Elliot grunted along with him. Donnie grabbed onto Elliot's cock and started pumping him in time with the thrusts.

Elliot cursed and gasped in so much steam Donnie feared he'd pass out.

"I'm gonna come," Elliot mumbled.

Donnie lost his rhythm, snapping his hips erratically as he neared the edge. He pressed in harder, filling Elliot up as he spilled. He tore Elliot away from the tiles and jerked him until he came, tightening around Donnie's cock in pulses.

Elliot's orgasm eased, and he let out a long sigh.

"It didn't hurt, did it?"

"As I've said the last twenty times we've fucked, no, it didn't hurt."

"Good. We can continue in the bedroom, then."

Elliot snorted. "Why not here?"

"I want to eat your ass, and I like to take my time with it."

"Bedroom, then," Elliot said, flashing a smile at Donnie over his shoulder.

****

Donnie woke alone.

It was a habit of Elliot's to leave the bed stealthily, one Donnie hated. He threatened to handcuff him to the bedframe, but that only seemed to excite Elliot, who did his best to goad Donnie into it. He rolled onto Elliot's side and took a deep inhale of his pillow. Elliot's familiar scent fluttered his insides. He rolled onto his back and twitched his nose at another scent coming under the door, something sweet. He climbed out of bed to investigate.

Elliot was standing in front of the stove wearing his tight boxer shorts and Donnie's shirt. Donnie stared at his ass as it flexed. Elliot was wriggling, whistling a happy tune. There was a plate on the side with a stack of pancakes.

Donnie approached him and wrapped his arms around Elliot. He looked over Elliot's shoulder to the frying pan and the browning pancake.

"Not gonna hit me with it?"

"Maybe later if I think you deserve a good spanking."

Donnie nipped his neck. "Would like to see you try."

Elliot laughed, turning off the gas. He twisted in Donnie's arms and smiled. His blue eyes burned into Donnie's, and he couldn't look away. There was so much trust and awe in the look, and Donnie knew he was looking at Elliot in the exact same way.

Elliot narrowed his eyes, and Donnie narrowed his in return.

"What?" Donnie asked.

Elliot wrinkled his nose, and Donnie readied himself for the words. The two words that had plagued him since they'd met. He tilted his head and schooled his expression into one of irritation.

"Morning, baby."

Elliot's voice was so soft, it took a few seconds for Donnie to register what he'd actually said. It wasn't his normal taunt, but something domestic, calm, and comforting.

It wasn't a taunt at all; it was nice.

Donnie released a pleased sigh. As a pet name went, he'd become fond of Elliot calling him baby, and the way he'd just said it, all happy, and sweet, made the butterflies in Donnie's stomach dance.

He cupped Elliot's cheek, kissed him firmly on the mouth, then pressed their foreheads together.

No more goodbyes, only lots of good mornings to look forward to.

The end.

FLOWERSHOP ASSASSINS

Bye Baby

So Pathetic

Raging Ranger

I hope you enjoyed Bye Baby, if so, a review would be hugely appreciated on goodreads and amazon

Thank you!

Louise <3

If you enjoyed Bye Baby, you might like some of my other titles:

Self-published titles:

Adrenaline Jake Series

The first in the novella series is free on amazon, and the second is free if you sign up to my mailing list: Sign up

Evernight tiles:

The Freshman

The Psychopath

[The Rat](The Rat)

Balls for Breakfast

New Recruit

One for Sorrow

[Two for Joy](Two for Joy)

Facebook group for teasers, updates, etc:

Louise's Lockup

Happy Reading

Louise <3

Printed in Great Britain
by Amazon